Note to Reader:

Three historical strands are woven into this story:

* *c.* AD 861 Vikings raided North Africa, taking slaves back to the north. These men were known as 'Blue Men', an intriguing name which lingers in today's Irish language.

* *c.* 880 Harald Fairhair fought a sea battle at Hafrsfjord against a rebellion of pirate kings from south-west Norway. At stake was the title of first undisputed King of Norway.

* Also around this time, Ohthere, the Viking explorer and trader, came to King Alfred's court in Wessex. The tale of his epic voyage to the uttermost north was recorded among the king's papers, the only Viking voice to have come down to us from the Dark Ages.

Julia Golding

OXFORD
UNIVERSITY PRESS

OXFORD

UNIVERSITY PRESS

Great Clarendon Street, Oxford OX2 6DP
Oxford University Press is a department of the University of Oxford.
It furthers the University's objective of excellence in research, scholarship,
and education by publishing worldwide in

Oxford   New York

Auckland   Cape Town   Dar es Salaam   Hong Kong   Karachi
Kuala Lumpur   Madrid   Melbourne   Mexico City   Nairobi
New Delhi   Shanghai   Taipei   Toronto

With offices in

Argentina   Austria   Brazil   Chile   Czech Republic   France   Greece
Guatemala   Hungary   Italy   Japan   Poland   Portugal   Singapore
South Korea   Switzerland   Thailand   Turkey   Ukraine   Vietnam

Oxford is a registered trade mark of Oxford University Press
in the UK and in certain other countries

British Library Cataloguing in Publication Data
Data available

ISBN: 978-0-19-272761-9

1 3 5 7 9 10 8 6 4 2

Printed in Great Britain by CPI Cox & Wyman, Reading, Berkshire

Paper used in the production of this book is a natural,
recyclable product made from wood grown in sustainable forests.
The manufacturing process conforms to the environmental
regulations of the country of origin.

For Edward, my Viking expert

And with thanks to the Norwegian voyagers,
Mum, Dad, as well as Clare, Pat, and Alan Bryden

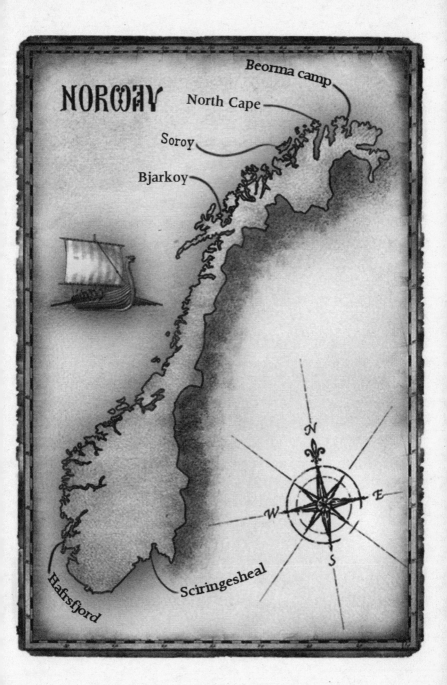

NORWAY

Beorma camp

North Cape

Soroy

Bjarkoy

Sciringesheal

Hafrsfjord

N

W E

S

Main Characters

Enno—known as 'Blue Man', an African

The Vikings
From Bjarkoy island
Freydis—daughter of a jarl or 'earl'
Toki—her older brother
Ohthere—their father, a jarl and richest man
   in the north
Magda—their old nurse
Sigtrygger—cook
Leif—Ohthere's right-hand man

Pirate Rebels
Sulke—captain of the *Marauder*, in blood feud
   with Ohthere
Kleppe—his second-in-command
Eirik of Hordaland—leader of pirate rebellion

The Sami Tribes
Finnas
Tapiola—head man
Tuoni—his grandson

Beormas
Aino—seventeen-year-old girl, bear keeper
Lempo—her twin brother
Pekka—their father
Chief Atcha—head man
Hero—a domesticated bear

The Return

'I have wielded a blood-stained sword
and howling spear; the bird
of carrion followed me
when the Vikings pressed forth;
In fury we fought battles,
fire swept through men's homes'

(Egil's Saga)

1

NORWAY, AD 880

With the sun in her eyes, Freydis could not see the distant ship skimming down the fjord like a many-legged spider towards a fly. She sat in the doorway of the farmstead enjoying the spring air, an embroidery frame on her lap. Bent over it in concentration, tongue tucked between her teeth, she bathed in the warm light that spilled into the hall. It made her hair shine like the creamy butter on the cool, dark shelves of the dairy and brought the design on the frame to life with vibrant colour. The canvas was almost finished, the product of a long winter on her home island of Bjarkoy, a season when the sun disappeared and the snow reached the roof. Gold knot-work wove through a border of animals—a red serpent, a black wolf with snapping jaws, a white-furred fox, a brown bear, a sea eagle with a fish in its beak—pictures inspired by her life here in the north.

As well as a few extras from her imagination, she admitted, smiling to herself. Something to make Toki laugh when he spotted them. She had included two dwarves with grumpy faces and a dragon with a curling tail among the other creatures.

'Freydis, come and see the newborn!' her brother called from the paddock. A loose-limbed reindeer calf staggered to nuzzle for milk like a drunkard at the Midwinter feast.

Only eighteen but already tall and broad-shouldered, Toki looked in silhouette against the shining water of the fjord very much like their father, thought Freydis as she pulled the thread taut. But his warmth, thank the gods, was all his own. He was delighted by the new addition, yet another proof that the herd was flourishing under his care. When their father returned—if he ever returned—it would be almost double the size it had been when he left.

'Come on, snail!' Toki called again.

'I'll come in a moment,' answered Freydis. 'Just two more stitches.'

With a final snap of woollen thread, she completed the pattern, a headrest for the jarl's chair, the seat of the lord of these lands. Mumbling rare words of praise, her old nurse, Magda, took it away to back with fine linen, ready to decorate the hall for that evening's meal. Freydis imagined Toki sitting at the head of the table, the embroidery, her gift to him, in pride of place.

'I'm ready now, Toki!' Freydis ran swiftly down the path worn between home and paddock, jumping the old drift of snow that sagged against the north wall in a dirty sprawl.

But Toki was no longer looking in her direction. He was staring out to sea at the square white sail of the longboat sweeping down on them from the iron-grey horizon.

'To arms!' he shouted.

2

In the corner of the silversmith's workshop, Enno was dreaming of his home on the North African coast. It was a good dream, bitterly sweet. He welcomed anything that took him away from this savage northern world where the sun hid his face for months on end and the mountains threw long shadows, a place where the ground was either boggy or covered in ice. He'd been trapped here so long he feared his blood was turning as cold as the many rivers that ran through the grudging fields to the sea.

The shop door banged open and a big Viking entered, brushing a light fall of snow off the Arctic fox fur cloak looped over his shoulders. Enno's master, the silversmith, stirred himself from his chair by the hearth and extended a hand.

'Jarl Ohthere! It's been a long time since we

last saw you in Sciringesheal. What can I get you today?'

The Viking released the brooch fastening his cloak and let the fur drop to the floor. A gold ring glinted on his upper arm, marking him out as one of the king's men. King Harald had summoned his faithful warriors from all over Norway to counter the rebellion of the pirate lords. With so many nobles in town, the shop had never been busier. Taking a step forward, the Viking clasped the smith's palm and shook hands. 'I've got some good skins, silk, and walrus ivory aboard the *Sea Otter*, all for trade. Are you interested?'

The smith smiled. 'Might be.'

'Then show me what you've got.'

With all the pride of a master craftsman, the silversmith reverently laid out his newest jewellery for inspection—colourful necklaces of glass beads twisted with silver wire, shining rings for arms and fingers, engraved medallions—wrought from materials from many countries, luxury goods fit for the very rich. He watched his customer's face, gauging his reaction, waiting for the glint of appreciation, the flare of greed.

'Of course, you may wish to commission something special,' the smith prompted. 'You aren't celebrated as the foremost man from Halogaland for nothing, Jarl. A little something to cheer the long winters up north—I'm sure you can afford it.'

Ohthere grunted. 'But I can't afford the time to wait for you to make it—king's orders.'

The smith nodded. 'Ah, you've heard then—about the rebels?'

'Aye. Much has changed and I've been away far too long—almost a year.'

'That's an impressive journey, Jarl. You must have travelled far.'

'Nearly all the way to the Golden City. We overwintered near Lake Ladoga before turning back. My crew are anxious to be home. Their wives won't be pleased to learn that we are duty bound to return to the muster once we've secured Bjarkoy.'

'I imagine not.' The smith caressed the blade of a silver dagger, discreetly bringing it to his customer's attention.

Ohthere pushed it aside. 'But perhaps their hearts will lift when they hear that the king has ordered us to hunt Sulke the Pirate—he's ours.' This was announced with relish and the Viking's stern face cracked into a bloodthirsty smile.

Enno shivered and wrapped his patched cloak more closely to his body. Fighting and feuds—the Norsemen had a bottomless appetite for both. Even Enno had heard of the enmity between Jarl Ohthere and Sulke the Pirate, a blood grudge between their families that had started with murder several generations ago and was renewed, rubbed raw, by fresh outrages every few years. Enno had no idea—nor did he care—who was to blame, but in truth with feuds that did not matter. After a time the hatred was so deep-rooted that it became as natural to the two families as breathing. And now this private battle was to be used as part of King Harald's larger struggle to hold on to power against the pirate lords of south-west Norway.

The smith nodded his head in understanding. 'Then you must not tarry. By all means, make your choice from what I have to hand. I would not wish to delay you.'

Silence fell in the murky confines of the shop. Smoke curled up to the ceiling from the central fire, before finding its way out of the vents in the shingle roof. Enno closed his eyes, listening to the sound of the birds calling outside, the softened thud of feet on the wooden walkway that ran between the merchants' houses, the clink of metal as the Viking stirred the goods on display with his blunt fingers.

'Who's that?' asked the Viking as he rifled through a pile of silver dirham coins.

Enno kept his eyes closed. He had heard too

many versions of this conversation over the years to care.

'Him?' The smith spat at the fire, spittle dying in a brief hiss. 'I got him from Domnall Seal's-head.'

Ohthere laughed, as if that explained a lot.

'They call him Blue Man,' continued the smith. 'He's been passed around the slave markets since he was a little boy—no master ever keeps him long.'

'Troublesome?'

'Finds it hard to accept that he's a slave. He has a bad attitude to work.'

'Where's he from?'

'He was taken captive after that raid on Italia.'

Ohthere released a handful of coins with a dismissive gesture.

The smith chuckled. 'They took a score of prisoners from the fabled lands of North Africa and brought them home as mementoes of their voyage. Can you imagine the stupidity? Men from the deserts sold as slaves for our climate! Half of them died the first winter.'

Ohthere snorted with disdain. 'Let me have a closer look. I've heard of men with such skin but never seen it with my own eyes.'

The smith waved him forward. 'You'll have to go to him, Ohthere. He gets conveniently deaf when asked to display himself. Waste of my money. I knew he wouldn't be much of a slave, but I thought he'd bring folk in to the shop; but what's the use of having a blue man if he doesn't show off for my customers?'

Enno felt a strong grip ring his upper arm as he was hauled to his feet. He swallowed his surge of anger. He'd long since learned there was no point fighting every battle for his dignity.

'You! Blue Man! Look at me,' ordered Ohthere, clicking his fingers under Enno's nose.

Reluctantly, Enno complied. He found himself confronted by pale blue eyes fringed by deep lines. The Viking was as tall as he, but broad-shouldered where he was wiry, ruddy-skinned where he was dark. There was something craggy about the man, like a weathered rock at sea that refuses to succumb to the battering of the waves. He looked old, well past forty, and he was swaying slightly, as if he had not yet recovered his land-legs.

Ohthere reached out a calloused hand and rubbed at the skin of Enno's forearm.

'It's real then—not paint?' Ohthere marvelled, eyeing the swirl of tribal marks on the young slave's cheeks.

'Aye, it's real,' agreed the smith.

'His skin is more black than blue, isn't it? Though I suppose in daylight it looks like that dark blue gleam you get on charcoal.' Ohthere shifted the arm higher so that he could see it better, his interest impersonal: the curiosity of a man who likes puzzles.

'I always thought it looked like the dyer's hands after he's been using the blue stain.'

'Aye, that's so. What if you cut it?'

Enno jerked back, pulling his arm free. Anger flashed across Ohthere's face. 'I'm not going to hurt you, fool!'

The smith tutted at his slave's behaviour but shrugged. 'Same as us—he bleeds red.'

'So why is he dark-skinned?'

The two Norse men pondered the mystery.

'You know, Jarl, I think he must have got scorched. His country is too near the sun,' declared the smith sagely.

'Maybe your country is too far away. You Norsemen are so white because you never baked properly.' Enno's voice was clumsy over the harsh sounds of their language but perfectly understandable.

His irritation forgotten, Ohthere laughed at the slave's boldness. 'I like him. Sharp—spirited. Can I buy him off you?'

The smith tried to look reluctant. 'But I'm just getting used to him. He's one of the family now.' He

12

patted Enno on the back with a show of fatherly affection that fooled no one. 'I know you are a great collector of curiosities but I don't think I can bear to be parted from my blue man so soon.'

'Clever words, Smith. You skilfully twist and beat them like silver to fit your purpose.'

The smith bowed at the compliment wrapped in the accusation. 'I could be prevailed upon to give him to you in exchange for a walrus skin. I take it you have walrus? I know a shipwright who's after some.'

Ohthere nodded, stroking his grey-streaked beard. 'Aye, the last tribute from the Sami people brought in some fine pelts. I'll give you two skins for the blue man and that cloak brooch.' He tapped a large silver disc etched with a ship that lay on the workbench.

'A gift for your son Toki?'

'Of course.'

'But rumour has it you've got a daughter too.'

Ohthere's face set in grim lines. He gave a curt nod. 'How did you hear about her?'

'I'm on good terms with your crew, Ohthere. They spoke of a little songbird by the name of Freydis Ohtheresdottir. A man's son provides comfort in his old age, but daughters bless his house in his prime. Can I interest you in something for your

13

girl?' The smith scattered a few decorative pins across the counter.

Ohthere frowned. 'At what price? Daughters are nothing but a drain on a man's purse.'

'Three skins for the brooch, a five-inch pin, and the man.'

The Viking considered the deal for a moment then held out his hand. 'Done. I'll send the skins over this afternoon.'

The smith shook on the agreement. 'Which pin?'

Ohthere wandered away to examine a filigree knife scabbard. 'It doesn't matter. You choose. Whatever you think a girl would like—Freydis is about sixteen now.'

The smith gave a crafty smile at the Viking's back. It was obvious to Enno that he was going to pick the least expensive to make up the purchase, but one in particular had caught the slave's eye: a long pin with a wolf's head on the nub. No admirer of his old master, Enno was determined the smith would not get away with too much profit from the deal.

'That one,' Enno said softly, nudging it with his fingertip.

'What?' The smith was no longer looking so happy.

'She would like that one.'

Ohthere returned to the counter. 'I agree. It's unusual. I'll take it.'

'Are you sure?' The smith's hand hovered over a plain round-headed pin.

'Yes. My new slave has good taste.' Ohthere picked up his cloak and handed it to Enno to carry, so confident of his own authority that he did not even check the African obeyed. 'What do you think, Smith? I might give Blue Man to my daughter as a bodyguard—I've never given her a slave before and Toki has plenty. It's about time she learned to manage one.'

The smith shook his head. He looked worried.

Probably wondering how he could have squeezed more profit from the deal, thought Enno sourly.

'No good will come of it, Jarl. He's spent his twenty or so years crafting himself into the most stubborn slave in Norway. Don't say I didn't warn you about his attitude.'

'You worry too much, Smith.' Ohthere pocketed the silver trinkets and beckoned to his third purchase. 'Come along, Blue Man. Time to head home.'

3

The raiders had gone.

Freydis used the knotted rope to haul herself out of the hole where she had been hiding, knocking a broken barrel out of her way. Blood trickled from the wound in her leg but she barely felt the pain. Her home was gone—all that remained was a skeleton of charred timbers marking the place where the hall had once stood. They were surrounded by the ruins of the sod walls that had not burnt so well in the inferno. Heat still radiated from the embers. The pirates had taken or slaughtered all the livestock, sunk the fishing boats, and stolen the food supplies before firing the barns. The devastation was complete.

Grabbing a broken broom as a crutch, she staggered slowly from body to body, her right leg dragging uselessly behind her. Each face in their little community was known to her. The house-karls had fought bravely but had been outnumbered. Even the women had taken up arms at the end—the weaver, the dairymaid, the midwife bearing pitchforks and spears—but they had either died or been taken. Only she had survived, thanks to Toki's quick thinking which had seen her thrust in the new pit privy Father had ordered dug in his absence.

But where was Toki? Why had he not come for her?

Freydis turned over another man, fearing to see her older brother's features staring back at her, but he was not there. Each revelation was both a relief and a blow. Old Hakon. Thorkil the One-Eyed. Aud the Fair. All dead.

The last body examined and Freydis knew that her brother was not among the warriors sent to Valhalla during the battle. That meant he was probably still alive somewhere, a captive to their enemies. Sulke the Pirate, an old adversary of her father's and the man who had led the raid, would surely know her brother's worth as son of the richest man in the north. Surely he would choose wealth over the blood feud between their families? There was hope that Toki might yet be ransomed.

A fool's hope.

In pain and overwhelmed by grief, Freydis stumbled and fell to the ground, giving way to tears.

A chill wind brought her to her senses, brushing her bare neck in a reproachful touch. Freydis swiped angrily at her eyes. Her fit of crying had changed nothing. Still the ruins of the hall smoked and her friends lay dead around her. She could not afford the time to grieve like this. If she didn't take action, she too would number among those lost that day.

She pulled herself to her feet unsteadily. The dark blue waters of the bay were empty of ships. The little island of Bjarkoy had been left in peace—for now. Around her, the gently sloping fields were green with new grass, apart from the vile black circles that marked the site of burned-out buildings. In the distance, on the larger islands to the south, the spruce-covered hills rose up to mighty Moysalen, the old man of the mountain range that rarely lost his white cap of snow even in the height of summer. There was no sign of any other human, friend or foe, for miles around.

A bolt of pain in her side as she shifted her weight reminded her that she had to see to her own wound. During the initial onset of the attack, the pirates had unleashed their dogs to track all who tried to flee. She could still hear the baying of a wolfhound, the nip at her ankles, followed by the agony in her hip as a raider had stabbed her thigh with his sword to stop her running, the impact jarring her whole body. Toki had killed the man but had had no time to treat the injury before bundling her into her hiding place. She'd already used a strip of linen from her under-tunic to bind her leg to a rough wooden splint but now the blood had seeped through and the knot loosened. Leaning against a sod wall, she unwound the cloth and bit back a cry when she saw the jagged cut for the first time in daylight. The wound was not bleeding much—Toki had once told her that if the blood pulsed from an injury like a heartbeat then the person would bleed to death—but she suspected that the bone was cracked or broken. Gritting her teeth, she wrapped a fresh strip around her thigh and hip, held rigid by the splint, and tied it off as tightly as she could. That done, she let her dress fall back and stood up as straight as the agony would allow, taking all her weight on her left leg. The wound probably needed to be cauterized to stop it turning bad, but that would have to wait.

What to do now? She was on her own in a ruined farmstead. All the food and livestock had been taken or spoiled—the people of Bjarkoy scattered or dead—there was no one to help even bury the bodies and those would soon attract the wolves out of the forest. In her injured state, there was no question of her being fit to undertake the difficult path over the mountains to the nearest neighbours—that was assuming they had escaped attack and would be able to aid her. There were no ships left in the harbour; not even a fishing boat. She knew better than to expect help from outside. Her father had been gone a year and they had had no news of the *Sea Otter*. He could even be dead and it would take many months for word to filter back to his family.

Feeling close to panic, Freydis took a grip on the amulet around her neck and prayed to Freyja, after whom she had been named, whispering desperate words, begging for guidance. The goddess of fertility was especially revered in these parts where it was so hard to grow crops; Freydis had always honoured her with harvest sacrifices and gifts thrown into her sacred springs. She didn't want to speak the thought out loud in case of offending the gods, but she felt it was time her devotion was rewarded.

Freydis waited, but no answer came. Still the wavelets lapped on the beach and the wind tugged at her clothing, but there was no change that could be interpreted as a sign, not even an over-flight of birds.

Clenching her fists, Freydis realized with sickening finality that she really was on her own. Her gaze fell on the twisted remains of what had once been Aud, a girl a few years older than her. Freydis only had to close her eyes to see how things had been, how they'd played together when they were younger, climbing on the rocks and gathering flowers in the meadows. Once they'd stolen the boys' tunics when they were swimming in the bay—the two girls had got into trouble for that particular joke. Now an axe-blow to the back of Aud's head had put a cruel end to her life, stopping all laughter and fun. Freydis could not bear to leave her friend like that, carrion for crows and wolves. But with no fuel to build a pyre or the strength to make one, the only grave available was the hole where she had hidden. It would have to do.

A sound behind her made her jump with alarm. Hooves. Turning, she saw one of the farm's domesticated reindeer trotting up the valley, a rope dangling awkwardly, catching around his feet. Scared off during the raid, the bull had returned and was now pacing regally towards Freydis, bending his head to snuff her hair. Comforted by the presence of another living being, Freydis leant her forehead to his nose, breathing in the familiar scent of the animal.

21

'Sorry, I've nothing for you,' she said, her voice sounding odd in the empty homestead, 'but you've arrived just in time to help me.' She took the halter and untangled it from his legs.

Trained to assist with the herding of the wild reindeer of those parts, the bull waited patiently.

'White Star, isn't it?' Freydis scratched the pale patch on his nose. He was one of her brother's favourites. 'Come.'

With the reindeer doing the heavy work, Freydis began the laborious process of dragging bodies into a mass grave. Numbed by shock, she did not question where she found the strength to loop a rope around each body. Even the pain seemed distant, someone else's problem as it shot up her right side with every swing of the crutch. Being small for her age, Freydis would never have managed the task if the pit had not been at the bottom of a slope, allowing the heaviest bodies to roll in under their own momentum. Once all had been pushed inside, she fastened the rope to the wooden cover and guided White Star so that he slid it into place. Then she placed as many rocks as she could reach on the lid to prevent it being moved by a wild animal. The wolves would still smell the dead but at least they could not get at them.

Straightening up, she leant wearily against

White Star and scanned the horizon again. Though nothing had changed, she was still in danger. She needed a fire at the very least to drive the wolf packs away from them both and attract a ship to her rescue.

With a bitter laugh, Freydis found one positive aspect to her plight: with the embers from the hall still glowing, she would at least have no trouble building them a bonfire.

4

The ropes bit into Toki's flesh. He tried not to groan but it was like being gnawed by the teeth of Fenrir, the great wolf from one of the skald's legends. Toki could barely feel his hands, as they were yanked behind him and bound at the wrists. He tried to find a more comfortable position, but there was none. This close to land, Sulke the Pirate had ordered that Toki be restrained, fearing that his prize would try to escape again as he had on the first night.

Toki remembered those first dark hours on Sulke's ship, the *Marauder*, with a shudder. In the aftermath of the raid, he'd been so desperate to get back to help his sister that he had risked everything on a mad dash for the side. The pirates had caught him, beaten him for his disobedience, then made sure he was under strict guard. The ship had sailed too far now for him to have any chance of returning in time to help Freydis, but the thought of her injured and trapped in that pit made him sick. Would she even be able to get out of the hole? Or would she die there alone and terrified? He was all she had—she needed him.

Rolling on to his back, Toki tried to lever himself upright. One of the pirates' wolfhounds sat watching him, drool spooling from its jaws to the floor. Grey and shaggy, the dog had a wild look, its gaze hungry, begging for the command to attack the human bound helplessly at its feet. Toki shuffled back; knowing better than to show fear around the creature, he gave it a cool glance then looked over its head. He no longer recognized where he was. A low line of islands, black on the azure water, floated like a fleet of longboats in front of a distant range of white-dusted mountains. The peaks glowed violet in the late afternoon light; clouds, tinged pink and purple, hardly seemed to move in a pale blue sky. This was a land beyond his knowledge—ethereally beautiful, a stark contrast to the squalid, ugly conditions on board the ship.

Toki's captor had sailed north after the raid, risking the open sea rather than the protected passage through the Tranoyfjord. The pirate preferred to arrive unannounced, swooping down on his next

25

prey from the least anticipated direction. Just as he had on Bjarkoy.

Searching for his enemy among the thirty or so men of the crew crammed on the warship, Toki fixed Sulke in his gaze, wishing he had the power to punish him. Even before the attack Toki had detested the man whose father had murdered Toki's grandfather—the beginning of the blood feud. Now his feelings had deepened into bone-deep hatred. Sulke was standing up at the bow, clasping the dragon figurehead as he balanced on the side. He was surveying the land for the presence of people, searching for his next victims. Of only medium height, Sulke made up for his lack of brawn by his ruthless skill with sword and knife. He could gut an opponent with the impersonal slice of a fisherman's wife preparing the catch. He wore his shoulder-length brown hair slicked back with whale oil, better to see his foes in a fight, he claimed, but it also made him look sleek, serpent-like, a deadly enemy in case anyone needed the warning. Toki found himself comparing his father, Ohthere, to Sulke: Ohthere's rages had always been hot, loud, and short-lived, like a summer thunderstorm; from what Toki had seen, Sulke's violence was bitter and cold, like a winter blizzard.

As Toki watched, Sulke shouted something

over his shoulder to one of his men. Whatever it was, it appeared to be good news for the pirates for Sulke was grinning broadly, teeth flashing white against his close-trimmed dark beard.

He'd laughed like that when he'd finally subdued Toki, the last man in Bjarkoy left standing to defend his father's hall. He'd taken the son in payment of an old debt, Sulke had explained, smiling all the while as if conveying a great favour on Toki. By the time Ohthere returned from his voyage there would be nothing left of his old life—no homestead, no son, no tribute from the Sami people. A plucked goose in place of the once proud eagle.

Toki closed his eyes, braced for the return of a wave of despair. How he wished his father was here now. The responsibility of caring for the people of Bjarkoy had been his, Toki's, whilst the crew of the *Sea Otter* had been away for the year. Even though he was only eighteen, his leadership had been respected by those left behind and in many ways it had been a happy twelve months. He'd felt as if he'd finally stepped out of the long shadow of boyhood and become a man. Though he loved and admired his father, he had always felt burdened by having Ohthere's high expectations focused solely on him. But left alone to act in the jarl's place, Toki had discovered that he could rule fairly, manage the farm and herds successfully, and look out for his sister.

Until the pirates.

In the space of one short day, he had managed to lose everything. Though he knew that he had not stood a chance with so many of their fighting men away on the voyage, Toki still felt the disgrace of his failure. And now his most fervent wish was for his father to come so Ohthere could both rescue and forgive him.

But Toki would never forgive himself if Freydis was dead.

'Boy! Toki Ohtheresson!' Sulke gave his captive a kick in the ribs to rouse him.

Toki opened his eyes and scowled. The pirate had been consistently mocking his youth ever since he had defeated him. 'What now?'

'What now, *master*.' Sulke's voice was deceptively smooth, the sheen on a polished blade.

Toki's frown deepened as he debated the consequences of refusing to use the title, but defiance was a point of honour with him. 'What now, Captain,' he said at last.

Sulke gave a grudging grunt of amusement. The lad had as stubborn a spirit as his cursed father, even when he was trussed up as awkward as a basking seal on land. 'Tell me what you know about your

28

family's arrangement with the Sami people of these parts.'

Toki hunched his shoulders, preparing for the blow. 'Tell me why I should aid my father's enemy?'

Sulke's right hand dropped to his knife hilt. 'That is easy. If you don't, I'll kill you—but before that I'll kill the other prisoners. Whose life shall I take first?' He lunged into the huddle of women by the stern rail, winding his fist in the hair of the nearest, Toki's old nurse, Magda. 'This one perhaps? A bit too old for the slave market.'

'Please, no!' she cried, her wrinkled hands clawing at Sulke's tunic.

Toki feared his face wasn't as expressionless as he would have liked. 'Let her go. If you hurt any of us, I'll not tell you a thing.'

'Good, for that means you will speak to protect your people.' Sulke let Magda drop as if she were of no more account than a soiled rag.

Toki could feel the attention of the people of Bjarkoy on him; his old nurse's grey-green eyes round with fear. She'd watched him as a child— making sure he did not fall in the fire or come to harm about the homestead; now she was seeing him lead them all across an impossible tightrope, death on one side and slavery on the other. Would she

29

condemn him for speaking or thank him for keeping her alive a little longer?

'I think you know already, Captain, that my father claims tribute as far as the island they call Soroy.'

Sulke nodded, indicating that he should continue with a flick of his dagger.

'The lands beyond are unknown to us—the land of magicians and strange gods. My father told me that the Sami people bring their reindeer to Soroy for summer grazing. They swim the herd across the sound from the mainland as there's plenty of reindeer moss and grass on the island.'

Sulke rubbed his chin in thought. 'How much do they pay for the privilege of your father's favour?'

'Usually four reindeer per family, depending on the size of the man's herd. Skins, feather, oil, and bones are also given in tribute but I'm not sure in what quantities.'

'And what do the reindeer men get in return?'

Toki shrugged. He hated being put in the position of betraying his father's business to his enemy. 'The chance to trade. Grain—because they cannot grow their own so far north. Iron goods. Protection. It is an old and respected exchange.'

Sulke used the point of his knife to dig some dirt from under his thumbnail. 'I'm sure your father thought so. The Sami are soon going to see the advantage of taking a new overlord. Kleppe!'

The giant of a man, black bearded and ruddy-faced, stepped forward. The planking creaked under his leather boots. 'Aye, Captain?'

Sulke tossed the knife so it spun in the air, then caught the hilt. With startling swiftness, he slashed the bonds at Toki's wrists. 'We're taking the boy with us. Keep him close.'

The pirates sailed their vessel into a bay that faced towards the sea, then splashed ashore in the shallows, leaving a skeleton crew and the other prisoners on board. Forced to disembark with the raiders, Toki stumbled along, prodded in the back by his minder if he went too slowly for Kleppe's taste. Seaweed caught about his ankles as he scrambled on to the grey sand; he tripped and fell into a rock pool, taking a mouthful of saltwater. Kleppe laughed at Toki's clumsiness and hauled him to his feet.

'Don't drown yet—we want the pleasure of killing you ourselves,' Kleppe mocked.

Climbing the low cliffs protecting the pasture, the raiders arrived on a plateau. In the distance, Toki could see a large herd of reindeer grazing amid grey rocks, dark faces with branching antlers low to the ground, white flash of their tails bright against the rusty green of the moss.

'Good.' Sulke rubbed his hands together and cracked his knuckles. 'The Sami have already arrived for the season.'

Sulke led the way as his men fanned out behind him, an arrowhead bearing down on the peaceful camp of the herdsmen. Toki spotted the ring of tents belonging to the Sami as he crested a rise. The dwellings were clustered around a central fire, and from this distance he could see women working around the hearth, clad in padded jackets over colourful dresses of red and blue, heads wrapped in scarves against the cold breeze. Small children played at their feet, the girls wearing miniature versions of their mother's clothing, the boys dressed in warm leggings and thick tunics, again in bright hues, with floppy cone-shaped hats. The cheerful scene lasted only a few moments before the presence of the raiding party was noted. A woman sounded the alarm, swooping down on a toddler and gathering him into her arms. Like a flock of startled birds, the Sami women scattered, fleeing towards an outcrop of rocks not far from the encampment and disappearing behind the stones.

'That's not going to help them,' laughed Sulke, finding the primitive defence of run-and-hide very amusing. 'Now let's see what their men do.'

The pirates didn't have to wait long in the

abandoned ring of tents. A small group appeared, running from the direction of the herd; another party approached from the sea, fishing nets slung over their shoulders. In a pincer movement, they converged on Sulke and his men, rudimentary weapons held ready but not yet in attack position.

The leader, an elderly man with a face lined like crumpled linen and deep-set dark eyes, stepped forward. A tall youth with long brown hair stood guarding his back.

'Strangers, what are you doing here?' the chief asked.

Sulke gave him a shallow bow, eyes never leaving his. 'Old Man, we come in peace. Will you not welcome us to your camp?'

'What kind of peace do you offer, armed with swords and spears?'

'The peace of wary men. Invite us to sit with you and I will explain.'

'You say you are wary—but I must be more so. Explain first—then maybe we sit.'

'All right, Old Greybeard, we will do this your way for now. My name is Sulke; I have taken over as Jarl of these territories. Here, as proof of my claim, I bring with me Ohthere's son, Toki.'

On cue, Kleppe pushed Toki forward on to his knees between the two groups of people. Toki's face burned bright red with humiliation. He kept his eyes lowered. A pair of reindeer-hide boots trimmed with scarlet braid appeared in front of him. A hand came to rest on his shoulder, warmth seeping through the thin wool of Toki's dirty tunic.

'Is this true, my son? Are you Ohthere's boy?'

'I am.'

'And your father, is he dead?'

'I . . . I don't know,' Toki admitted.

Sulke stepped forward. 'But his hall is gone—I made sure of that. Ohthere the Traveller, if he returns, will come back a man of no renown, power-less and poor—a name that will become dust as he has no child to carry it on after him. Trust me, Old Greybeard, when I say he will be forgotten and the name of Sulke the Slayer will live on. I am taking over whatever arrangement you had with Ohthere. It will be to your advantage to accept this swiftly before I reconsider the level of tribute I levy on you and your people.'

'And what would that be?' the old man asked heavily.

Sulke flashed him a ferocious smile, all teeth. 'I am sure you are wise enough to know that you must foster the friendship of a lord such as me; brambles and weeds grow on the little-trodden way. My price is eight reindeer each man.'

34

'Eight!'

'Eight.'

With stooped shoulders, the chief backed away. 'Let me talk with my brothers.'

Sulke gave him a wave of permission. The leader retreated into a huddle with his people, breaking the bad news of the high tribute in the sad fluting tones of their language. Toki remained on his knees, grit digging into his skin. He could see that the long-haired youth was putting up a spirited resistance to the idea of giving the pirates so much. Toki silently urged these gentle tribesmen to accept the demand without argument as he had seen at Bjarkoy how rapidly Sulke exacted revenge on those who crossed him.

The debate did not take long. The leader returned and ceremoniously placed his fishing spear on the ground at Sulke's feet.

'Come, Jarl Sulke, sit at our fireside. My name is Tapiola. You and your men are welcome.'

The pirates exchanged grins at conquering without having to strike a blow. Proudly, they took the best seats on the stones ranged around the fire. Unnoticed now his job as symbolic victim was done, Toki got to his feet and retreated to the entrance of the nearest tent. As he watched the Sami hover around their new masters, he could not help but

35

sympathize with their plight. They tried to hide their resentment, but the leader's expression was strained as he beckoned three women over to return to cooking. In this harsh world of the barren north, survival depended on knowing when to bend. Of the few trees to survive up here, the stunted pines and birches bowed to the wind rather than fought it. They were probably counting on the fact that Sulke would not stay—he would go and they could melt back into the great wilderness of the north, fleeing to places where the pirate could not hunt them down.

They were lucky.

THE CHASE

'He who makes blades bound,
the warrior wont to rule, supposes
our fate's in his two strong fists;
that's to be expected.
But I guess that before he gets me,
the ring-giver, craver of sword-crashing,
will meet with tricks'

(THE SAGA OF REF THE SLY)

5

On board Ohthere's ship, the mariners were talking excitedly, calling to each other like a colony of seagulls. After three weeks at sea, the familiar landmarks of their home coastline were coming into view—steep-sided mountains rising out of the dark waters of the fjord; inlets leading to sloping meadows grazed by sheep, goats, and reindeer; pink-headed gannets with black and white plumage fishing from seaweed-fringed rocks. A few hardy trees clung to impossible ledges, barely a cupful of earth to hold their roots. Every few minutes, another waterfall was revealed, swollen by snow-melt, plunging down sheer rock like veins of silver in the grey stone.

Enno crouched near the starboard rudder in the stern of Ohthere's cargo vessel, *Sea Otter*, listening to the exchanges. He had spent the voyage trying to glean information about his prospective mistress, the daughter that Ohthere had mentioned. From past experience, he knew better than to expect a female to be any kinder than a man; if she was anything like her father, she would be harsh and uncompromising. Viking women, though not counted equal with their menfolk, could still be formidable types.

Enno rubbed the markings on his cheek, remembering the pain of a particularly firm slap from a glassworker in Birka. His old mistress had run her workshop with an iron fist and sharp tongue. They had not fared well together and it had been a mutual relief when Domnall Seal's-Head had taken Enno off her hands. He was not expecting much joy from this Freydis, but he found it infuriatingly difficult to find out anything about her. Ohthere's conversation was all about his son, Toki; if Freydis was mentioned, the men merely smiled. She seemed well enough liked, reputed to be the most cheerful girl in Halogaland, but of little account to anyone, especially to her father. To be the slave of someone so unimportant to her own community would make Enno the lowest of low, another slap to one who had once been the son of a wealthy man in his own land.

Enno first realized something was wrong when the mariners fell silent. They were staring at something over to the port side—a wisp of smoke, a grey smudge against the twilight sky. Shading his eyes, Enno could see that someone had built a bonfire on the strand but there was no sign of habitation; the place looked abandoned, a collection of charred sticks.

Suddenly, Ohthere roared a command for the oars to be manned. With the smoothness of a well-practised crew, the mariners took their places on the rowing benches and added the power of the sweeps to the steady progress they had been making under sail. Even the master was putting his back into the effort.

'Blue Man! Get your arse on the seat and row!' Ohthere ordered through gritted teeth when he saw that Enno had not moved.

Deciding there was no humiliation in rowing like a galley slave when even his master was doing so, Enno took his place at a free oar. The trading vessel skimmed over the last few hundred yards to the little beach, the men grimly silent. Once the keel crunched on the shingle, the sailors shipped oars, grabbed their weapons and jumped into the shallows. Enno watched in confusion as all but one of the crew ran off, leaving the ship, crammed with valuables, exposed on the shore.

'What's happening?' he asked, but the old sailor left behind to mind the *Sea Otter* hushed him

41

with a slashing gesture. He then pushed Enno in the small of his back, indicating that he jump ashore and tie the ship to the wooden posts further up the beach. Grabbing a rope of twisted walrus skin, Enno did as he was told, stumbling on the pebbles that slid beneath his bare feet. He wondered just what was going on. Whatever homecoming the crew had expected, this was clearly not it.

Then a scream rent the air. A girl. Acting on instinct, Enno dashed back to the ship, grabbed the nearest weapon and raced towards the sound.

Freydis had been sleeping by the bonfire for two days. The wolves had not ventured into the homestead, though she'd heard their haunting cry from the forest, a song that tugged at her heart. White Star had stayed by her side, grazing only a few feet away, a familiar sight that made the ruins less lonely. She took comfort that his liquid brown eyes were calm when he raised his head to scent the air, his branched antlers proud against the pale grey clouds.

The fire crackled, sending sparks wheeling up to the blank skies. Freydis shifted uneasily. The initial burst of energy in which she had managed to deal with the bodies had passed, leaving her suffering from a low fever. She shivered as she lay by the fire, wrapped in all the scraps of sack and cloth she could salvage, a tattered, shapeless mound. She passed her time dreaming of warm food and kind words and tried not to think about what would happen to her: the prospect was bleak for a lone girl—and an injured one at that—unless a friendly ship came calling.

Without warning, the night exploded. Men attacked from all sides, weapons raised. Terrified, Freydis let out a scream—the raiders had come back, they were going to finish what they had started—leave no survivors to tell tales! Unable to stand on her injured leg, she sat up, shedding layers of sacking, and groped around for a weapon, but found only stones and sand under her fingers. Throwing handfuls of anything she could reach, she shuffled back to the fire, sobbing with terror.

'Stop!' A man yelled at full blast, bringing the attack to a sudden end. 'That's no raider!'

Freydis threw one last handful towards the sound and covered her head with her arms, waiting for the killing stroke at the back of her neck. May it be swift and sure, she prayed. But then hands seized her and lifted her out of her nest of rags. Freydis panicked, fighting like a mad thing to escape. She would not let them take her—not like they

43

took Toki and the others. She kicked, scratched, and bit.

'Stop it, child.'

Freydis went limp. Her father. This was a stroke of good fortune beyond any that she had anticipated. He'd returned. At last.

'Papa?' she whispered, realizing now her panic had lifted that it was indeed his smell of salt and leather, his chest that she was crushed against. 'You came.'

He held her firmly away from him, looking her over. She could feel his arms trembling. 'You're injured?'

She kept her eyes on the amulet around his neck. 'I think my leg is broken.'

'What happened? Where's Toki? Who did this?' His eyes were now scanning the shadows as if expecting his son to stride out to greet him. Someone did run forward, but it was not Toki. Freydis thought she must still be dreaming when she saw the black-skinned young man brandishing a spear, firelight revealing the warlike circles tattooed on his cheeks.

'Put the weapon down, Blue Man!' ordered Ohthere angrily. 'There's no one left to fight.'

The dream became even more strange, for this other-worldly creature obeyed without a word, dropping the spear at her feet. How had her father managed to tame this dark elf to do his bidding?

'Freydis, tell us everything from the beginning,' ordered Ohthere, giving her a little shake to drag her attention away from the elf-man. He looked around for somewhere to place her, wanting to distance himself from his daughter. She moved first, reaching for White Star's rope bridle and supporting herself against the reindeer's warm flank.

The crew stood in silence as she haltingly recounted the tale of the attack three days earlier. Pain stabbed up her injured leg but she forced herself to endure. It would have seemed disrespectful to sit when her father was on his feet. She felt as if she was on trial.

'Who did we lose?' Ohthere asked towards the end of her account. She could sense the anger in him, beating against his control like stormy waves on a harbour wall.

Freydis stumbled through the names of the six people she had buried, frantic not to make a mistake. She was fully aware that it was the deaths of the kinsfolk of those before her that she was reporting.

'And what happened to the rest?' Ohthere's eyes had turned cold; he was looking at her as if she were a stranger to him, one he didn't like very much at that moment. He had said nothing to congratulate her on her quick thinking about dealing with the bodies, not a word of sympathy for what she had endured. The warmth and relief she felt on his arrival had rapidly cooled to a familiar icy dread. Despite a year apart and the disaster that had befallen them, her relationship with her father was falling into the same old pattern where she could never please him.

She twisted her hands in the cloth of her skirts. 'I didn't see what happened, Papa. I think they were taken prisoner by Sulke. Toki is probably among them.'

As her words confirmed his suspicion, Ohthere let out a howl of fury and grief. 'Toki! My son! My son!'

The raw pain in his voice was too much; Freydis closed her eyes, blinking away the tears that threatened to spill. She couldn't be sure Toki was still alive, but if he was, how would he survive the harsh treatment on the pirate vessel under the control of a man who hated all of her father's blood?

Ohthere turned to his crew. 'We will hunt them down. That Hel-cursed pirate will keep my son alive only as long as he sees any use in him. We leave immediately.'

'But what about your word to King Harald that

you would return swiftly?' asked Leif, his second-in-command, stepping in his path.

Ohthere thrust him aside. 'Harald said Sulke was mine. My orders are to secure the north. We can't do that with the traitor preying unchallenged on our lands.'

'True.' Leif backed down. 'Toki and our people should not be abandoned.'

Freydis hung her head, swaying against White Star as a tide of dizziness washed through her. On her other side, an arm cupped her elbow, steadying her, cool against her hot skin. She looked down to see dark fingers wrapped around her pale inner arm. Strangely, she no longer felt frightened of the elf-man; his touch was reassuring, unlike her father's harsh expression.

'Your daughter is suffering, Jarl Ohthere.' The one her father had called Blue Man was speaking with an odd accent but his words were plain. 'She is injured. You must see to her needs first.'

Freydis raised her eyes to find her father considering her with something like disgust.

'Injured! This is an evil jest—look, men, how the gods leave me a feeble girl in place of a healthy boy!' Closing the distance between them, Ohthere took her chin in his hand and pulled her head up. 'Why did you survive when my son was taken?'

47

Freydis swallowed against the lump in her throat. 'I . . . I don't know, Papa. Toki saved me. He made me hide.'

Ohthere released her. 'He should have hidden with you—or fled. He is too young to match himself against a foe like Sulke.'

'I'm sorry, Papa, but I couldn't stop him. There was nothing I could do.'

'"Sorry" is not going to bring my son back. Can you tell me which way Sulke went?'

Freydis shook her head.

'Then you can be of no further use to me.' Ohthere turned from her. 'Leif, lead a party to the outlying farms and find out if anyone knows where the raiders were headed. Sigtrygger, take the rest of the men and salvage what you can.' He straightened, his eyes sweeping the wreckage of the harbour and hall. 'I grieve with all of you who have lost family in this cowardly attack. Have no doubt about my resolve: we will avenge them.'

Ohthere gone, Freydis hugged herself, trying to warm the cold place in her heart frozen by her father's words. She'd been so relieved by Ohthere's unexpected return but now she wished she'd died before he made shore. She'd always known that she was of little importance to him—the sun rose and set on Toki in their household—but never before had Ohthere so publicly spurned her.

'Grief makes men bitter,' murmured the stranger at her side, easing her down on to her pile of rags. 'They turn on those things closest to them, hurt most those they love.'

Freydis did not have the energy to argue that her father didn't love her, that he only spoke the truth when he said she was of no value to him.

'Let me see to this wound, little one.' Fingers gently probed at the cut. 'You tended this yourself, yes? All this time? You did well. It has not gone bad and your fever is slight. I will cleanse it with water and put on a new bandage, then you must rest until the body has time to heal itself.'

Freydis lay on her side, letting his words ripple over her.

'So clever to bury the bodies—that too was well done of you.'

Her eyelids felt heavy. She let them close, knowing that as long as that deep, dark voice continued to talk, she really was safe.

6

As the short night dimmed to grey—it would never be truly dark this far north even at midnight, not until autumn returned—Enno sat on guard beside his new mistress. She looked so frail in the firelight, pale and thin, worn down by pain. Her curling blonde hair had been pulled into a rough braid, but strands had escaped to stick to her feverish skin. Her features were delicate, the opposite to the harsh features of her father—nose tip-tilted, long fair lashes, a sprinkling of freckles. Perhaps pretty once she was cleaned up and had a smile on her face again. Her light grey-blue eyes were closed now. Kind eyes, which surprised him, considering whom she had as a father. From the look of her, it was unlikely that she would last long in this harsh place—a fact that could be good news for him as slaves were often freed on the death of their master or mistress.

No, not that. Enno slapped away the thought of her dying as he would a troublesome fly; it had been buzzing around in his head ever since he'd seen the seriousness of her wound. He couldn't wish that fate to befall the girl even if it would benefit him. He'd admired her spirit, standing up to report to her father like a soldier to a commanding officer, despite being on the point of collapse. Her courage and quiet strength had called to something in him. He suspected that she, like him, had spent many years battling against the odds: she against her callous father, he against his enslavement.

Remembering the scene, he cursed Ohthere under his breath for his hard heart. The girl had clearly wanted her father's embrace and a promise that all would be well; instead she had been listened to in judgemental silence and told that she had no right to hide when her brother had not. What was wrong with these Vikings that they had no love for their own kin?

His little mistress stirred in her sleep, a moan escaping her chapped lips. He trickled water into her mouth, pleased to see her swallow it. Yes, she'd survive if he had anything to do with it.

What was he thinking!

With an abrupt change in mood, Enno tossed the canteen of water aside in self-disgust and bunched his fists. He had vowed long ago never to care for any of these northerners; to attain his goal of returning home he had to keep from making ties to anyone or any place, always looking for his opportunity to escape. And now he had caught himself acting nursemaid to a girl, lured into committing himself to protecting her just because she was weak and vulnerable. He could not afford to soften.

Boots crunched over the pebble beach, approaching quickly.

'How is she? Is she well enough to travel?' Ohthere asked, squatting down at his daughter's side.

'She is unlikely to be able to walk without pain again.' Enno was no expert on wounds but he thought the bone had not set properly—no surprise when she'd had to tend it herself. 'You should get someone to cauterize the cut before it turns bad and make her a proper splint.'

Ohthere ran his hands wearily through his hair, dislodging the leather cap that protected his skull. 'You think the gods will leave me one child? What good is a crippled daughter?'

'I think your gods have less to do with her recovery than the girl herself.'

'Aye, she's proved more stubborn than I

expected—but I have no use for daughters. I've always said it was a shame she wasn't born a boy.'

'She is as God wills, Jarl.'

'True, the gods decide our fates. But we have no time to wait for her to heal. I'll send Olaf with the iron—best do it while she sleeps.'

Ten minutes later, Enno watched in sick silence as the ship's smith heated a poker in the hottest embers of the fire. He'd seen a fair number of wounds sealed this way but that never made it any easier. Waiting for Olaf's signal that all was ready, he undid the bandage, bracing his young mistress so she could not flinch.

He thought later that he would have given a year of his life not to have heard her scream before she passed out with shock and pain.

Wrapped in a blanket, Freydis huddled at the stern of her father's ship. For the past few hours, she had turned in on herself as she struggled to come to terms with her sudden change of fortune. With their home destroyed, Ohthere had had no choice but to take her with them as they set out on their pursuit of his son and the raiders. He made it clear that he would have preferred to leave her behind.

The search party led by Ohthere's right-hand

man, Leif, had reported that Sulke the Pirate was rumoured to have gone north. It made sense. If Sulke wanted to strip Ohthere of everything, rub his nose in his losses, he would go in search of more riches from the Sami people whose tribute was the foundation of Ohthere's wealth. The Sami provided the Vikings with skins, feather, and bone hunted in the cold lands above the Arctic Circle. Skilled trappers, boatbuilders, and reindeer herders, these people lived in uneasy alliance with Ohthere in return for protection and bartered goods; but with Ohthere's homestead destroyed, the signs indicated that Sulke thought he could take over this arrangement just as he had Ohthere's people and goods. It was probably what would be keeping Toki alive: Sulke could use him as the key to open the Sami treasure chests to him.

Freydis knew her father was determined to retrieve Toki and as many of the captives as he could, as well as punish Sulke for his attack. Wasting no time, Ohthere had buried much of his valuable cargo in the ruins of the homestead, left behind a small crew of men to begin the process of reconstruction, and was now travelling light and fast, hoping to gain on the four day start the pirates had on them. And she went with them like a small bundle of unwanted luggage.

It was a strange fate to be travelling so far on the strength of a rumour, Freydis reflected, as she watched the woollen sail billow in the wind. The world was so huge that Toki could really be anywhere, but she understood why her father had to put his faith in Leif's information. She wanted to believe it too.

And she didn't want to give up hope either. When she closed her eyes, she could see her brother's face with its habitual smile. Big and sandy-haired like her father, Toki was very different by nature—sunshine and laughter to Ohthere's stormy moods, eyes warm and approving rather than angry and assessing. Toki was impulsive, quick to like people, swearing that his instinct was never wrong. All the girls in Bjarkoy had hoped he would fall in love with them but he'd sworn he'd know his soul mate when he found her—and she didn't live on his home island.

It was Toki who had made Freydis's childhood a pleasant memory as, with a dead mother and a father who preferred to ignore her existence, no one else would have cared for her. Father and son did share a love of travel and curiosities though—both with a thirst to discover what lay over the horizon. Toki would have enjoyed meeting Blue Man, questioning him about his homeland and experiences.

Freydis's new slave crouched at her side, whittling a piece of whalebone with a small curved knife. Her father had told her gruffly that morning that the stranger was hers. Another change she had to get used to—she'd never been responsible for another person before.

'What's your name?' Freydis asked him, noticing for the first time that the young slave's brown eyes were fringed with thick curling lashes. They gave little away as to his real thoughts.

Enno paused in his task, surprised by her question. They'd been at sea some hours now and she had not spoken to anyone, least of all him.

'They call me Blue Man,' he replied.

'Is that the name you were given at birth?'

'No.'

'So what is your real name?'

'That belongs to my old life. Blue Man will do.' Enno resumed his carving.

Freydis watched his hands competently turning the bone, shaping it into a reindeer's head. His difference from her was fascinating—even when his skin was covered in goosebumps. She had a strange impulse to smooth them, but didn't dare.

'You're cold?'

'I'm always cold.'

'It's a warm day for early spring.'

56

'You think it is warm; I know it is cold.'

She tucked a stray strand of hair behind her ear. 'You don't speak like a slave.'

'That's because I am not a slave.'

Freydis choked on an unexpected urge to laugh. This was so clearly not the case. 'Er . . . Blue Man, you may have missed it but my father gave you to me.'

'But I did not give myself to you. What he did does not matter between us.'

She frowned. 'Yet you serve me.'

'It suits me to look after you—that is all.'

'And when it suits you not to do so?'

'Then I will tell you.'

Freydis was speechless. She'd never met a slave like him. She wondered if she should tell her father what he had said but she feared it would lead to Blue Man being punished. 'Well, at least I know where I stand,' she said in a joking tone.

'Yes, you do,' he replied seriously.

Freydis let the silence return. Not wanting the stranger to be punished, she could only hope to persuade Blue Man of the realities of their relationship by experience and, as he was obeying her for the moment, this would have to do.

She turned her gaze to the cliffs of the fjord passing rapidly by. Under any other circumstances, she would have been excited by her first voyage. All her life up to this point had been bound by the limits of Bjarkoy but now they were heading into unfamiliar waters. The ship was threading its way through the narrow passage of the Tranoyfjord, using the protection of Senja Island to avoid the more perilous route north on the coast exposed to the open sea. Though they were sailing as fast as they could, she felt frustrated by their progress, knowing that every moment counted against Toki's chance of survival. Lying back on the sacks that formed her seat, she spotted a sea eagle shadowing their vessel, hovering motionless overhead like a black rune scratched on a white stone. What did it see from up there? A broad-beamed sailing ship drawing a white wake through the fjord as a bone needle pulls thread. Was the bird a good omen? The gods were so hard to read.

Her father was standing at the rudder watching the same eagle. He had aged ten years overnight—the lines on his forehead deepened as if carved there by Blue Man's whittling knife. A light fall of rain dampened his hair against his neck. As Freydis watched him, she felt a mixture of tenderness and longing for the man who barely noticed her.

No, it was worse than that, she admitted. He resented her because he had never been convinced she really was his child, keeping her very existence quiet like some shameful family secret.

But surely that shouldn't matter now? Dare she take his hand? They were both suffering: would he accept her comfort for their shared loss?

Before she could make a move, Leif came to relieve him. The stocky Viking passed Ohthere a waterskin.

'Watch the current, Leif,' Ohthere muttered as he relinquished the rudder. 'It's tricky around this headland.'

Leif nodded but bit back the usual banter he would have made about his superiority as a sailor. Everyone on the crew had lost someone in the raid and no one was in the mood for light-hearted exchanges. Grim and businesslike, the men all applied themselves to the pursuit with single-minded determination.

Freydis waited in hope but Ohthere did not choose to sit near her. He perched on a cask where he could keep an eye on the horizon, then took out a cloth-wrapped package from his pocket. Gently shaking something loose from the linen, he folded his fist round it and held it to his chest. She caught a glint of silver but could not see it clearly. What was it that he hugged so close to his heart—something vital to him?

'Papa?'

'Hmm?'

'What's that? May I see?' Freydis pointed to the closed fist.

Reluctantly, Ohthere opened his fingers, revealing a circular brooch in the design of a ship under full sail. He gazed at it wonderingly, as if seeing it for the first time himself.

'Oh, it's beautiful!' Freydis exclaimed, reaching out to touch it.

He snatched it away. 'It's for Toki.'

'Of course.'

Ohthere folded the brooch away and shoved it back into his pocket. 'You can't have it.'

'I didn't ask for it.'

Ohthere ignored her. He was filled with so much pain, he barely knew what he was saying, just felt compelled to release some of the poison inside him. He couldn't bear his false daughter sitting there when Toki was in chains.

He stood up, towering over her. 'I bought you a slave—is that not enough for you, Freydis? No? You're just like your grasping mother.'

'My mother was not grasping,' she said with quiet dignity.

'How do you know that? You don't even remember her. She died bringing what she claimed was a seven month child into the world. But what was she doing nine months before you were born while I was at sea, eh? Can you tell me that?'

Freydis shook her head.

'Playing me false, that's what.'

'She did no such thing.'

'How do you know?'

'Toki said. I was small—born too early—I'm yours.'

Ohthere waved a dismissive hand. 'Believe what you like. I know what I know. Toki was the only decent thing that woman ever gave me.' He threw a smaller, thinner cloth-wrapped parcel at her feet. 'Here, open this—I was persuaded against my better nature to buy it for you. Strangely enough, it suits you.'

She shrank away, trying to make herself a smaller target for his wrath. 'I don't want any-thing—'

'Take it! That's the last thing you'll get from me. Now Toki's not here, don't think you can just step in and seize what is rightfully his.'

Freydis gulped, her focus blurred as she stared at the silver wolf pin lying on the deck. It was

61

magnificent but hardly a flattering comparison. 'I wouldn't dream—'

'Of course, you would. It's all clear to me now—you are the only one to benefit from the raid, aren't you? With Toki out of the way, you're left my only heir—men will offer for you even as you are— but I'm sure you knew that when you hid and let the others be taken.'

Freydis had already been knocked down emotionally by her father's rejection of her; this felt like a kicking as she lay in the dust. His description of her thoughts was so far from the truth, it would have been laughable if she hadn't wanted to cry.

'I don't want—'

'But it won't work out like that. I kept you for your brother's sake, you know—even if you're not mine, I can't dispute you had the same mother. I'll find Toki and then things will be back as they should be. You'll gain nothing, you understand?'

Freydis swallowed against the lump in her throat. 'Yes, Papa.' How could he believe she could possibly wish anything to happen to Toki?

'It's the blood of your mother's people in you.' Ohthere continued to rant, talking himself into a skewed view of her motives. 'Rabid wolves, the lot of them! Bad blood.'

Freydis shuddered. But she didn't believe her

blood was tainted, because that would mean Toki's was too. No, her father was wrong.

'I see it in you—hiding, sneaking when the others were out fighting.'

'You . . . you would have preferred me to fight?' She rubbed her hip unconsciously.

'It would have been the honourable choice.'

Enno couldn't believe what he was hearing: Ohthere was berating his small-framed girl as if she were a soldier who had thrown his sword aside and fled the battlefield, not a faerie-like creature with no more place in a fight than a butterfly. Grief had obviously sent the man mad—no sane father would talk to his child like that. As for his accusations that she was illegitimate, they were ridiculous. Her features were his in miniature; he only had to look in a glass to see the truth.

Enno stood up, fists clenched at his sides.

'Jarl Ohthere, look at your daughter!'

Ohthere's head snapped round at this unexpected interruption. 'How dare you address me like that, slave!'

Enno shook his head slightly, refusing to be distracted from the matter at hand. 'Look at your daughter. She is . . . how old? Sixteen?'

Ohthere nodded curtly.

'How can you blame her for doing the only

sensible thing in the middle of a battle between grown men—on the order of her brother, no less?'

Freydis was astonished: the stranger defended her at his own risk, standing between her and her father like a shield. His courage made her feel valued, worth something, for the first time since the pirate attack. Her Blue Man had become her champion.

Ohthere's wild grief swerved to the new target. 'Keep out of my affairs or I will have you lashed for your impertinence.'

Enno shrugged off the threat. 'You're angry because you know I'm right.'

'I'm angry because you, slave, do not know how to talk to your masters! Sit down!'

Enno felt a hand tug at his tunic. He dropped his gaze to see Freydis looking up at him, terrified that he was about to be punished for the sin of defending her.

'Sit down—please!' she whispered.

Enno could withstand Ohthere's shouting but he could not resist her desperation. He crouched at her side, glaring at the six feet of unreasonable Viking looming over them both.

'Gods! What did I do to deserve these two?' Ohthere stabbed a finger at the pair. 'A rebellious slave and a cowardly daughter.'

Leif's voice broke into the argument. 'Is that a sail, Ohthere?'

His anger at Freydis and Enno immediately forgotten, Ohthere swung himself up on the side of the ship, clinging to the rigging as he shaded his eyes against the spray. 'Where?'

'Two points to starboard—but no, sorry, I was mistaken. A rock only.'

Freydis glanced over at the man on the rudder. The dark-haired second-in-command would have heard every word of their discussion. As Ohthere groaned with disappointment and leapt back to the deck, Leif risked a wink in her direction. She gave him a tremulous smile in return.

'Here.' Enno picked up the wolf-headed pin and placed it on her palm. 'Such a pretty thing should not be spurned.' He flicked his gaze to her father. 'It isn't right.'

7

When the greyness of night gathered around the
camp fire, the Sami chief, Tapiola, graciously gave up
his tent to Sulke the Pirate and his men to sleep.
Tapiola invited Toki to share a blanket with him and
his family in a temporary shelter they had con-
structed among the nearby rocks, but the new jarl
insisted on keeping his prisoner with him.

'Do not be offended, Old Man, but I do not yet
trust you,' Sulke declared. 'I see your weakness—you
don't like others to suffer and you pity the boy. But
he's nothing to you—it's your own people you
should worry about. If the boy gets away due to any
action on your part, they will suffer.' The threat was
made all the more impressive by the reappearance of
Sulke's favourite knife, which he flipped lazily from
hand to hand.

After that, the invitation to Toki was not

repeated and he was left with the pirates. Kleppe dragged him into the conical tent and tied him to a pole opposite the entrance. Without even a blanket, Toki was left sitting upright while his captors snored at their ease, wrapped in their furs. Confident that the Sami posed no threat, the pirates set only a single guard. Toki's sleep was fitful, his neck lolling at a painful angle, but he was determined not to show any sign of suffering. His pride in his ability to endure was all he had left to sustain him.

In the small hours of the morning, during one of his uncomfortable periods of wakefulness, the drumming started. The sound came from the direction of the rocks, like a steady heartbeat. At first Toki wasn't sure what he was hearing; it throbbed low, like the pounding of blood in his ears, certainly not enough to wake the sleepers. But when the guard stood to check on the disturbance, Toki knew he hadn't been imagining it. The pirate stuck his head out of the tent and pulled it back in with a curse.

'Hel-spawned magicians,' he growled, touching the rabbit paw amulet he wore round his neck. He sank back on his furs, taking no further action.

Toki leant his head against the pole, letting the beat of the drums ripple over him. *Magicians*. The Sami did have one power that the pirates feared: their fame as wielders of magic. They were said to cast spells to make the fields and rivers fruitful, to speak to the guardians of the wells and forests, and charm wild animals to do their bidding. He hoped their skills would protect them now. The drumming signalled the start of a ceremony; they were probably asking their spirit guides what to do about the visitors. Toki had always felt an insatiable curiosity about the lives of others; he wished he could see it for himself. His father had told him about the Sami shamans who drummed their way into the spirit world. They penetrated the beginnings of all things with music, which they used like a staff pushed through ice to reveal the depths beneath. The shamans saw the roots of mountains, the seed of the tree, the drop that made the river.

Through the open flap of the tent, torches moved among the rocks, soft voices called, the scent of herbs wafted in the air. A singer joined the drummer. His voice rose and fell in a simple melody, gliding between notes. A chant. A spell? Toki closed his eyes, wrapped in the enchantments winding round the camp. He could feel the air was heavy with magic, he could sense it brushing his skin with the touch of moth wings. The land was waking; the waters running; the breeze whispering in answer to the shaman's song.

Sleep claimed him.

* * *

At dawn, Toki woke with a start when Sulke threw back the closed tent-flap.

'Who was supposed to be on guard?' he roared, kicking the man stretched out across the entrance. 'You, Torolv?' Not waiting for an answer, he stepped on him to walk outside. 'Nidhogg's teeth! They've gone!'

The pirates emptied from the tent like mead from a spilled cup. In the slice of the outside that Toki could glimpse through the 'v' shaped opening, he could see the cold embers of the fire, empty stone benches, and flattened ground where tents had once been pitched.

'Good for you,' he muttered, congratulating the Sami on their cunning in escaping soundlessly during the grey darkness of night. Schooling his features to give no sign of his pleasure, he braced himself for the backwash of Sulke's anger. It was sure to come.

'Torolv! I'll slice you throat to belly for this!'

The unfortunate guard dived into the tent to seize his sword, springing up like a fox cornered by hounds as his irate captain stormed through the entrance.

'Don't you go blaming me, Sulke. It's those

69

magicians. They must have cast a spell on me. I can't fight their dark powers—none of us can.'

'That's dung, Torolv.' Sulke swung his weapon; his opponent brought his blade up to parry the blow.

'Ask the boy. He heard the magic too. I saw him—he was awake when it started.' Backing away, Torolv practically tripped over Toki's outstretched legs.

Sulke swung his sword round to rest the point on his prisoner's breastbone. 'Tell me what happened!'

'They held a ceremony last night,' Toki said hurriedly. 'I don't know what they did after because I fell asleep.'

'See, the enchantment worked on all of us!' Torolv declared, desperation making his voice crack.

'I don't believe in magic—not from these reindeer herders leastways,' spat Sulke. 'But I do believe in lazy guards.' With the strike of a snake, he spun and sliced off Torolv's left ear. The man gave a scream of agony, dropping his sword to clutch his hands to his head. Blood poured between his fingers. 'Maybe that will stop you listening to such stuff. Next time, it'll be your throat if I catch you asleep on the job again.'

Kleppe stepped into the tent, paying the sobbing man no attention. 'What now, Captain?'

Sulke sheathed his sword with a clunk as it sank into the wool-lined wooden scabbard. He looked momentarily lost for ideas, his own arrogance having proved a costly mistake with these Sami.

'If we chase, they could slip through our fingers like water,' Sulke admitted. 'But I haven't come all this way north to give up now. I need a hold full of walrus ivory to satisfy our allies that we can pay our way in the battle against King Harald.'

They were plotting against Harald Fairhair, Norway's overlord? Toki hadn't realized that Sulke had any ambitions above self-enrichment. This was treason. There had been rumours that some leaders of the petty kingdoms, the so-called pirate lords like Sulke, were dissatisfied with King Harald's dominance; it seemed that he and the other captives had the misfortune to find themselves in the midst of a rebellion.

Kleppe made no comment, just waited for the decision that he knew was coming.

Sulke grabbed his cloak from the ground. 'We pack up and head on to the next camp. I won't make the same mistake again. Forget the tribute. We take what we want and leave no survivors. The Sami need to learn the lesson that I cannot be cheated by a coward's trick like the one they pulled last night.' He turned to Toki and gave him a kick in the ribs. 'Your father did not teach them to fear us Vikings, boy. You will pay for his leniency with your miserable life if I don't get what I want from these reindeer men!'

Toki had guessed that blaming him in some fashion would be part of the aftermath. He kept his eyes fixed on his bound feet.

'Take him back to the boat. I'll deal with him later.' Sulke stamped away, kicking an abandoned cooking pot from his path so that it hit the rocks with a bell-like clang.

8

Enno was pleased to see that Ohthere's callous treatment of his daughter had one good result. The crew of the *Sea Otter* started to go out of their way to cheer up the girl when they thought her father wasn't paying attention.

About time too, he muttered to himself as he put the finishing touches to his whittled reindeer. It shouldn't be left up to an outsider to defend her.

Sigtrygger, a bluff, round-faced Viking, who had lost his hair early in his third decade, had been designated cook for the voyage. He created his meals on board, using a large bronze cauldron to contain the fire. He spent the evening hours crouched over the kettle, his bald head gleaming with sweat and his long blond beard tucked in his belt to stop it tumbling into the food. He reminded

Enno of the dwarves who made such vivid characters in the tales woven by the Norse skalds—jealous craftsmen poring over their handiwork, hissing if anyone dare come near. But fortunately, Sigtrygger was generous with the results once he had finished. He made sure Freydis got a prime serving of the dried-fish stew fragrant with angelica and laced with strings of edible seaweed.

Others also stepped forward to show her kindness. The second-in-command, Leif, told her some new jokes, gathered on their year-long voyage, and for the first time, Enno heard the light laugh of his mistress, but it was quickly stifled so as not to offend her father. Some of the signs of strain relaxed on Freydis's face as she dared to smile. Enno realized he had been right: she really was pretty, but also fragile, like the blossom that even now was being blown from the budding fruit trees.

That night, when it was finally too gloomy to risk sailing further, they anchored in the lee of a seal-shaped island. On a hint from Leif, some of the crew petitioned Freydis to entertain them. A lap harp was dug out of storage below deck and handed to her. She tried to refuse, discouraged by Ohthere who was brooding at the bow of the boat, but the men would not give up.

'We need something to lighten our hearts,

sweeting,' urged Sigtrygger. 'These are grim days for us all.'

Succumbing to the combined pressure of twenty men calling for their favourite tunes, Freydis began to play. Enno listened, spellbound, as she sang one of the tales he liked best, the creation of the world from the body of Ymir, the frost giant. After killing him, Odin and his brothers, Vili and Ve, made the sea from the giant's blood, the earth from his flesh, and the mountains from his bones. Finally they took his skull and made the sky. Enno didn't believe the story—and doubted that any man there did—but as long as the enchantment of the song lasted he could not help seeing the cold blue waters of the fjord and the arch of the sky as parts of one great frost giant.

Staring up at the grey clouds, Enno chewed reflectively on a hang-nail, tasting the lingering salt from the fish he had eaten earlier. No one really knew how things came to be; perhaps this song was as good an explanation as any other. Usually, he found the stories of the Norse gods lacking in reverence as they cheated, drank, and fought their way through life like a bunch of quarrelsome Vikings.

But perhaps that was the point, he mused, they were like the people they represented; not beyond and above their knowledge like the God his own people had taught him to believe in. He was grateful that he had been given teachers during those early years of captivity; two brave men, Am and Kas-Jalfir, who had taken it upon themselves to act as guides and protectors to the confused boy ripped from his own family. They had been murdered in Ireland when their piety had provoked the wrath of a local chieftain. That had marked the beginning of Enno's own solitary journey in the hostile world of the Vikings—the true moment of his exile. He had always embraced the terrible beauty of Am and Kas-Jalfir's sacrifice, keeping it like a shield between him and the northerners, a bulwark against compromise and a reason to keep himself aloof. Reminding himself of it now was the reinforcement he needed to stop one girl creeping through his defences.

When Freydis laid the harp aside, the men murmured their appreciation.

'Excellent!' Leif declared. 'If you had been born a boy, Freydis, you could have made your fortune as a skald.'

Freydis shook her head. 'Oh no. I could never hope to match Thorkil—he knew more songs than anyone.' Her voice trailed away as she remembered how she had last seen the family skald when she buried him.

Leif gave her a one-armed hug. 'He would be proud of you now. He taught you well.'

She forced a smile. 'Thank you.'

'Come on then, sing some more. How about Thorkil's saga about Ragnarok? His songs should not be forgotten, particularly now he's gone.'

'What!' protested Sigtrygger as he carefully banked the fire in the cauldron. 'That's all a bit morbid. I don't think I want to be reminded how we're all heading for a great defeat in the last battle.'

Freydis laughed, nudging the cook with her toe. 'That's not it at all and you know it! Thorkil always said there was nothing more inspiring than Ragnorok, one generation sacrificing itself to make way for the next and a world renewed.'

Sigtrygger grinned. 'Aye, he did, didn't he? How I miss the old rogue.'

'So do I,' admitted Freydis. 'So I'll sing his song—and no complaints when I fluff the lines. I'm not him, remember, just his pupil.'

Enno listened to the exchange with interest. These men—no relatives of Freydis as far as he knew—were taking the time to restore the girl's confidence. It was a side of Norsemen that he had not seen before.

It was a shame that some of that attitude did not rub off on the father.

As if on cue, Ohthere strode the length of the vessel to dump his bedding roll by the rudder. Freydis lifted her fingers from the harp strings, the last note humming into silence.

'Tomorrow, we should arrive at the Sami summer camp on Soroy,' Ohthere announced to the company, making no mention of his daughter's performance. 'If our enemy has come this way, they should be able to tell us. Leif, Olaf: take the first watch.'

His words were the signal for all to turn in for the night. Without waiting to be asked, Enno wrapped a sheepskin around Freydis before settling down at her side. A quiet hour passed but he could tell she was only pretending to sleep. He had an urge to talk to her, to hear her voice again when it was just the two of them.

'Your leg hurting you?' he whispered.

'Yes.' She paused, but the night made it easier to confess the thought that had bothered her all day. 'And I'm . . . I'm afraid.'

'Afraid of what?' He wanted to reach out and touch her cheek to comfort her but dared not.

'Something's wrong. My leg is really weak.'

'You must give yourself time. Breaks don't heal overnight.'

'But what if my leg never heals properly?'

Enno thought this very likely, but it was not what she needed to hear now. 'You sing well.'

'Thank you.' She accepted the change of subject. 'Do you sing?'

'Like a bullfrog.'

This earned him a snuffle of laughter. 'What kind of songs do your people have?'

'I . . . I don't remember,' he lied.

Disappointed, Freydis settled to sleep while Enno recalled the sound of the pipes and drums played by musicians in his village. It drifted through his memory like ragged clouds blown by a breeze—nothing whole or substantial, just an impression of celebration and blood-pulsing rhythms. He couldn't share that with her—didn't want to. The Vikings had taken so much from him; he held it as a point of honour not to give them even so much as a memory.

The next morning, the *Sea Otter* anchored in the sound dividing the island of Soroy from the mainland. Freydis stood watching the waves breaking on the little grey-white beach, thinking about the tenderness Blue Man had shown her the night before. He was an extraordinary person, so fierce on the outside, but kind and generous when you looked more closely. Just having him nearby acted like the warmth of the fire in winter, mellowing the pain of her wound, driving out the coldness of her father and even helping with her grief for Toki.

Smiling now, she lingered, admiring the cunning of an otter that was fishing from a rock, and so she happened to be the first to spot the Sami boy in his little boat of hide stretched over birch withies. He paddled it skilfully, darting between rocks so that his approach was disguised until the last moment.

'Papa, to starboard!' Freydis called.

Seeing that he had been sighted by friends, the boy waved and steered his boat directly towards the *Sea Otter*. Leif threw him a rope to secure his vessel and helped him aboard. About Freydis's age, the boy had long dark hair, dark eyes, and the ranging pace of the stag as he strode up the deck towards the jarl. He bowed to Ohthere.

'Jarl, Chief Tapiola sent me.' He spoke their language fluently with a sing-song intonation, gliding over the words as if they were notes to a tune he had learned.

Ohthere clapped him on the shoulder. 'Welcome. Tapiola's grandson, isn't it? Do you have news of my boy?'

'Aye, sir. He's with a man called Sulke. They came to our camp three nights ago.'

Relief swept Freydis: Toki was alive.

'Where are they now?' Ohthere asked.

'I don't know, sir. I was left behind to watch for you in case you were in pursuit. Grandfather said to bring you to our new camp. He'll have better information from his scouts than I can tell you.'

'Then take us there.'

'If you would take your ship across to the mainland, I'll lead you to the stronghold.'

The Norsemen hauled the boy's boat aboard and took their places on the rowing benches, not bothering to wait for a favourable wind for the short passage across the sound. The boy was given food and drink and invited to take his ease in the stern. He accepted both gladly and wandered up to the end where Freydis was seated. He gave her a nod and sat down across from her, not encouraging conversation.

But Freydis couldn't contain her questions. 'You saw Toki?'

The boy took a bite of bread and chewed. 'Aye.'

'Was he . . . was he all right?'

He put the bread in his lap and uncorked the skin of mead. 'You his kinswoman?'

'His sister. Freydis.'

The boy poured some of the drink into a cup and added a splash of water. 'He wasn't injured. Didn't look too pleased to be a prisoner, but who would? Those Rot-cursed pirates don't make kind hosts.'

This was no more than what Freydis had feared. She was just so thankful to hear that her brother was in one piece. 'What's your name?'

'Tuoni.'

'Nice to meet you, Tuoni.' She held out a hand.

Surprised, Tuoni leant forward, bridging the space between them, and shook it briefly. 'You know, Freydis, Vikings don't do that—offer someone like me their hand.'

'Perhaps I'm not like most Vikings then.'

'No, I think you're all the same underneath.' Tuoni swigged the watered-down mead. 'Our chief says your father is a good man, trades corn for a fair price, but I can't see much difference between that pirate and Jarl Ohthere, except that the pirate asked for more.'

She frowned. 'So why are you here now?'

Tuoni shrugged. 'Orders. Besides, I didn't like seeing your brother tied up like a beast. Could've been me.'

Enno approached softly from behind Tuoni, stopping to crouch beside Freydis. On seeing the African, Tuoni spat out his mouthful of mead.

'What in the n-name of Ukko is that?' he choked.

Enno gave him a thin-lipped smile.

'This is Blue Man,' said Freydis. 'He's from the south where the sun burns very hot. All his people are like this, they say.'

Tuoni eyed the young man suspiciously, still not convinced he was human. 'All of them?'

Freydis nodded, suppressing a smile, enjoying this small revenge on the rude Sami boy. It was funny how quickly she had become used to Blue Man's presence, his face the one she sought out in the crew just for the pleasure of looking at him.

'Does he . . . does he . . . ?'

'Do I bite?' Enno flashed his white teeth. 'Only sometimes.'

Tuoni reached out to touch the raised marks on Enno's cheeks, before thinking better of it. 'Wondrous. I want some of those. How did you do that?'

Enno couldn't honestly remember how he'd been given the marks on his cheeks; it had been done when he was still an infant.

'You have to undergo a painful trial by fire and water,' he improvised. 'The agony is beyond anything you can imagine. If you are worthy, God gives you the marks of a warrior.'

Tuoni nodded, believing every word. 'Wondrous. Can you show me how?'

Enno smiled inwardly at this fledgling fighter, liking his spirit. 'Maybe, if I judge you fit for the honour.'

'Wait till Chief Tapiola sees you. He's going to be so impressed. I wonder what your spirit-guardian is.'

'What do you mean by spirit-guardian?' asked Freydis.

Tuoni gave the Viking girl a grudging look. 'We all have one—a shaman can tell you what it is if he enters the other world to see your spirit in its pure form.'

'What's yours?'

'The sea eagle.' Tuoni pulled a piece of walrus ivory carved into the shape of a bird from under his tunic. 'I see far and fall on prey without a sound.'

'I suppose it's better than being a goat,' mused Enno.

'Nothing wrong with being a goat,' said Tuoni staunchly. 'My cousin Jumala has one as his guardian—it means he is sure-footed in the moun-tains.'

'And eats everything,' Enno muttered.

Tuoni frowned. 'Do you mock us, Blue Man?'

Enno sat back on his haunches, considering the question with a touch of shame at his behaviour. Why was he making fun of the boy's beliefs? 'Sorry. I was wrong to make light of these matters,' Enno said graciously.

Tuoni accepted the apology with a stiff nod. 'You'll learn better when you meet our chief.'

Enno did not reply, but he thought it unlikely that these men of the far north could teach him anything. The further from his home he had travelled, the more bizarre the beliefs. He longed for the simplicity of his own faith where you prayed to one God, not this multitude of spirits and deities.

'What do you think my guardian would be?' Freydis asked. While Enno had been dismissing the Sami's beliefs, she had been enjoying the new idea, silently allocating a creature to each member of the crew, fitted to their character.

'I don't know you so I couldn't say,' Tuoni said. 'You should ask Chief Tapiola if you want to find the answer.' He gestured to her hip. 'What's wrong with you?'

Freydis's gaze slid to the horizon. Enno stepped in.

'She was injured in the raid on Ohthere's hall.'

Tuoni raised his eyebrows. 'She was there—and survived?'

'Yes.'

'And the injury?'

'A raider's sword made a mess of her leg.'

'She's lucky to be alive.'

'Aye, that's true.'

So nice of them to discuss her good fortune as if she wasn't there, thought Freydis, feeling the misery she had been holding off nibbling at her control. This was her future—for everyone to ask what was wrong with her, why she couldn't walk properly. No one would ever wonder what she did right. Life was harsh in the lands of the midnight sun, even crueller to those who had any disability. From now on, she was going to be regarded as a burden to her people.

'Will she be able to climb?' asked Tuoni. 'Our camp is on a plateau. The only way in is up a cliff path.'

'No, I can't climb. I'll stay with the ship,' said Freydis.

Tuoni shook his head. 'It's not safe—your father will be too far away to help if the pirates come back.' He turned to Enno. 'We carry our old folk up at need. You'll have to do the same for her.'

'That is no problem. She weighs very little.' He rather liked the idea of having an excuse to hold her.

The last thing Freydis wanted was to arrive in the Sami camp marked out as a cripple.

'Then I'll climb,' she said tersely.

'No, you won't,' countered Enno with equal firmness.

'I'll manage.'

'No. I'm carrying you. End of debate.'

Tuoni watched the power struggle between slave and mistress with fascination.

'Er . . . who exactly is in charge here?' he asked, amused.

Enno shrugged. 'She's a bit stubborn, this one.'

'*This one* is your mistress, Blue Man,' Freydis replied, aware that her first experiment as slave-owner was rapidly turning into a disaster. If her father heard how she could not even gain the respect and obedience of the man he had given her, she would be in yet more trouble. 'I expect to be obeyed.'

'Not when you are talking nonsense,' Enno replied calmly. 'You can't walk; you certainly can't scramble up a cliff.'

'I . . . I can try. I used a crutch before.'

'Why try when you have him to carry you?' asked Tuoni reasonably.

Freydis could tell that they both thought her protests foolish. They didn't understand how she felt, how she needed to prove that she wasn't useless, particularly to two perfect young men like them. She got unsteadily to her feet and moved away, using the side of the ship for support. She hated her injury, hated what she had become, yet a traitorous part of her wanted to have a reason for letting Blue Man hold her.

Behind her, Enno spoke again.

'It's been hard on the little one,' he explained to Tuoni. 'Losing her brother, being hurt.' He was silent about her father's scorn, though he knew that that was the deepest cut of all.

Tuoni dismissed these things as easily as if they were swan's down blown on the breeze. 'She should be grateful she's alive and free.'

But I'm not free, fumed Freydis. I'm trapped in a body that may never work properly again. No one will want me now.

Tuoni and Enno changed subject, discussing what Sulke the Pirate would do now that he had been thwarted of tribute. A puffin paddled by before diving down to fish. Her attention distracted from her own plight, Freydis watched the water where the little bird had disappeared, waiting to see if it had been successful. It bobbed up to the surface, a silver fish in its multicoloured beak.

Her mood was too much like self-pity, Freydis decided, turning back to the ship, to the men straining at the oars. She needed to bob up to the top again, not stay down in the depths. If Enno wanted to carry her, then so what? She needed to adapt to her shortcomings, not wish for what had been.

She approached Enno and Tuoni. 'Blue Man, you may carry me to the camp.'

'Your wish, mistress, is my command,' Enno said with mock-gravity.

Freydis sighed. 'Why don't I believe you?'

'Because you are very intelligent.'

Tuoni laughed.

9

'It's no good, Sulke: there's no sign of anyone in these godsforsaken lands!' the pirate's second-in-command, Kleppe, complained. The big man adjusted a line on the sail, making the woollen cloth snap in the wind. The ship increased in speed, spray skimming the rail and wetting the decks. 'We've been at this for days and seen not even a wisp of smoke to say the Sami are anywhere nearby. Perhaps no one lives this far north. Look at it—the land's as barren as an old witch's teat!'

Toki had listened to similar grumblings for many hours. Kleppe was not the only one on board the pirate ship to think that Sulke's dreams of finding riches up here an illusion. He watched the waves as a lone rock came into view to starboard; it stuck out of the water like a staff, every ledge crammed with nesting kittiwakes. The stink of droppings and the shriek of birds defending their territories could be detected from a mile away.

'They must be here.' Sulke thumped his fist into his palm for emphasis, beating the invisible Sami. 'I've heard tales of at least three tribes amongst these northerners—the Finnas, the Beormas, and the Terfinnas—they can't all just disappear. There must be some sign of them somewhere. Get the boy.'

With a silent groan, Toki braced himself. He'd been beaten on return from Tapiola's camp. His nose was probably broken and his right eye blackened. He knew he had a death sentence hanging over his head and had no desire to do anything to invoke it.

Kleppe dragged Toki forward and dumped him at Sulke's feet. Toki could hear the worried mutterings of the other captives.

'Where've the Sami gone?' Sulke's question was accompanied by a kick.

Toki hugged his ribs. 'I don't know—truly I don't know. My father never brought me on a voyage this far north.'

Sulke grabbed a fistful of hair. 'But he must have told you something about the people—you are his son, the tribute would have been yours some day.'

Toki blinked against the pain inflicted on his

scalp. 'He told me that he stood as protector to the Finnas—Chief Tapiola's tribe is part of this group. The other Sami people you mentioned—the Beormas, the Terfinnas—he said that they lived further off, but they are wild. Kill Norsemen on sight. He never landed in their territory. It lies east of the world's end beyond North Cape.'

Sulke released his grip, shoving Toki from him. 'He may have feared them, but I don't. We'll make landfall and go in search of these savages, pull them out of their hiding places like a fox from a hole.'

Bad idea, thought Toki desperately. Ohthere had been careful never to sail further than North Cape because few travellers returned from the land that lay to the east at this northern edge of the world. The Beormas were reputed to be able to shape-shift and fall on their foes in the guise of bears; their magicians could command the elements and lead ships into bewildering fogs. They would make no distinction between captive and pirate. They counted all Norsemen their enemy, if the tales were to be believed.

Kleppe had other objections in mind. 'This is madness, Sulke! The other leaders are meeting in little over a month. If you want to be in on the battle with King Harald like you said, we have to turn back now if we are to make it to Hafrsfjord in time. You won't get anything if you turn up too late.'

Sulke went toe-to-toe with the big man. In a flash, his knife was between them, point to Kleppe's belly. 'Are you questioning my authority?' he snarled.

Kleppe looked down at the blade in disbelief. 'Gods, Captain: you know you don't need to ask that. I've been with you since we both made our first kills.'

'I take nothing for granted, Kleppe, not even your loyalty. That was why you made me your leader.'

Kleppe shrugged his bull-sized shoulders and gave a wry smile. 'True—and I know you'd stick that in me if you really thought I'd turned against you. But I haven't—I just want to make my point. I'm thinking it—they're thinking it,' he nodded at the crew, 'we should turn back.'

The knife dug a little deeper, making an indent in the man's belly. 'No.'

Kleppe was undaunted. Despite everything, Toki couldn't help admiring the man's courage. 'We've got the loot from Ohthere, slaves to sell; you could ransom the boy. That'd cover our share and more of the campaign.'

'I don't want to share, Kleppe, I want to lead—and to do that I need something rather more impressive than a bunch of worn-out female slaves and children.'

'But the boy—'

'That's personal.' Sulke sheathed his dagger. 'I want Ohthere to know his only child serves me until I see fit to cut his throat. It is the perfect vengeance for the years of insult heaped upon my family by those of his blood.'

Kleppe shook his head and picked up a length of rope to stow away. 'Ohthere's got his daughter still—if she survived.'

Toki fixed his eyes on the deck. *If* . . .

'What! There's a girl?' Sulke snapped, outraged that this detail had escaped him.

Kleppe stopped what he was doing, amazed to find his leader was not all-knowing. 'I thought you had to have heard about her, seeing how you've made it your business to destroy Ohthere. One of the women told me—that old one over by the rail. Freydis, I think the girl's called. Ohthere's only daughter.'

Ice creeping up his spine, Toki couldn't believe Magda had betrayed them, but Kleppe was pointing straight at her. She kept her head bowed. As the oldest of the women, she had only her knowledge of Ohthere's family to bargain with to stay alive.

'I wanted no one, no one, you hear, of that man's blood to survive!' shouted Sulke.

Slow to grasp just how furious his leader was, Kleppe returned to his ropes. 'Maybe she did, maybe she didn't. You've got the son—that's what matters to Ohthere.'

Swift as a lightning bolt, Sulke struck Toki across the face to gain his attention. Kleppe dropped the line he was holding, warily watching the storm unfold. Crew members shifted subtly out of Sulke's way.

'Boy, where's your sister? Is she hiding among the slaves?' He strode to where the women and children were huddled, searching for a candidate. 'How old is she, Kleppe?'

'Fifteen, sixteen—what does it matter?'

'It matters because the job is not done if she still lives.' Sulke rubbed his chin. 'A girl—can't you see: that changes everything!' He glared at the prisoners, ready to tear each one apart to hunt down the missing daughter.

'She's not here,' Toki rasped, his throat dry. He'd not been given anything to drink for hours. 'She died in the attack.'

Sulke quickly reviewed in his memory the bodies he'd left in the homestead. There had been a young woman—he remembered regretting

the waste as she would have made a good slave—
but he had the impression that she was older
than sixteen. 'You lie. We left no one that age
behind.'

'No, I'm telling you the truth. Freydis was
injured. I hid her in a bolt-hole but she won't
have . . . ' Toki bit down on his anguish, ' . . . won't
have been able to get out by herself.'

Sulke studied his face for a moment, then
burst into cruel laughter, the storm of his rage dis-
persing in sudden harsh sunshine. 'You are telling
me the truth, aren't you? I could have used her if she
lived but maybe this way is even better. Ohthere will
discover the body of one child and mourn the loss of
another—a double blow.'

Sulke swung round to address the crew. 'Right,
here's the plan, lads. We'll give it another two days. If
we can't rouse these Sami from their hiding place,
we'll turn back, raid another Norse settlement to
make up our shortfall, offload the slaves, then pro-
ceed to the meeting place with the rest of the fleet.
Agreed?'

'Aye, agreed,' rumbled the men.

Finally, Kleppe gave a nod.

'So let's make the most of this wind,' continued
Sulke, 'and round the North Cape to see if these
Beormas deserve their fearsome reputation.'

The crew scattered to attend to their tasks. As Sulke passed Kleppe, the big man hooked his elbow.

'You know you only have the boy's word about the daughter. The woman I spoke to seemed to think the girl was still alive.'

Toki looked up, hope flaring that perhaps his old nurse knew something he didn't. Had Magda seen Freydis escape?

Sulke nodded. 'Aye, but if I'm any judge of a man, the boy thinks she's dead.'

Kleppe shook his head. 'Fortune's so fickle: I only believe someone's gone when I see the body. So, what if she's not?'

'If the girl survived then I'll hunt her down. None of that man's seed will escape me.'

'And then?'

Sulke clapped Kleppe on the back. 'I know that you have no more love for Ohthere than I since his men killed your brother.'

Kleppe glowered at the mention of the rooming inn brawl in Sciringesheal that had deprived him of his sibling. Thanks to the feud, Sulke's crew and Ohthere's regarded it as their duty to fight whenever they met. Since losing his brother, the blood grudge had become personal. 'You know I want to kill Ohthere myself.'

Sulke shook his head in amazement. 'You do

not understand the subtleties of revenge, my friend. Of course, we kill Ohthere—but only after we've taken everything from him. Suffer first, die later.'

'A knife in the gut causes plenty of suffering.'

'But not as much as seeing your son slaughtered and your daughter used to build another man's power. Think, with Toki Ohthersson out of the way, the girl is the only heir to her father's land and wealth.' Sulke waited for Kleppe to work it out, but the man's brain was not as quick as his own to grasp the consequences. 'Look, if I marry her, I'll have a sound claim to his estate.' Sulke kicked Toki, well aware that the boy was listening in seething silence to every word. 'Ohthere will hate that, won't he, slave? Not that he'll have long to mourn the loss. I just want him to live long enough to realize what I've done.'

'You'd marry the wench?' Kleppe asked. 'Not enslave her?'

'Aye. Marriage is the quickest way to get to the land and title. No one would dispute my claim with both males out of the way.'

'You devious whoreson.' Kleppe's tone was admiring.

Sulke grinned. 'I know. If I'd heard about her earlier, I'd've made sure we left Bjarkoy with her alive—she would've made a better prize than all these captives put together. A dynastic marriage like that would have put me in a dominant position with our allies—no one else could match my wealth and holdings.' He shrugged. 'Too late now, but it might be worth calling in on young—Freydis, wasn't it? On our way home. That's if she's still at Bjarkoy above ground rather than rotting under it.'

Toki clenched and unfurled his battered fists, squeezing his anger until he had it contained. He hated the fact that Sulke's words made him grateful for an instant that Freydis was in all likelihood dead—better that than wedded to the monster before him. For once, Ohthere's reticence to acknowledge his daughter had done her good. His enemies had missed her. Toki had somehow to make sure they did not get a second chance. Escape was more urgent than ever.

10

Freydis arrived in the Sami stronghold on Enno's back. After fleeing the pirates, the herdsmen had retreated to a hanging valley, a natural fortress, carved by a glacier high on the side of the mountains. The path up had been every bit as difficult as Tuoni had promised, following the banks of a waterfall as it leapt and tumbled like a shoal of thrashing silver salmon down to the waters of the fjord. Once they reached their destination, they discovered a shallow valley with room for grazing, stone outcrops where the Sami camped, and a peaceful herd wandering the spring grass. Freydis was enchanted: it was a secret kingdom, a hidden world, where the Sami could live like gods with the Middle Earth of men spread out at their feet.

As Enno turned to check on the position of the ship anchored in the channel below, Freydis saw over his shoulder the sea beyond Soroy Island, merging with the horizon, a dark grey fading to pale skies. Spits of rain blew in her face. The rocky skerries protecting the mainland from the ocean appeared from this height as no more than giant stepping stones across a pond.

'I didn't realize the world was so big,' she said, half to herself.

'And I didn't realize you were so heavy,' replied Enno, letting her slither to the ground, regretting he had to relinquish her.

She smiled, having become familiar with his sense of humour. She was a light-weight, but even that had made it a struggle to transport her up the steep path they had just climbed.

Their arrival had attracted the attention of Tapiola's tribe. The Sami rushed from their tents to greet the newcomers with gifts of water and food.

'They seem to like your father,' Enno commented, watching an old woman kiss Ohthere's hand and press a piece of dried reindeer meat in his fist.

Freydis gave a crooked smile. 'Yes, he can be quite charming. He's helped them out over the years when they've had trouble with other less peaceful tribes, or when greedy Norsemen have come calling.'

'And they've just met Sulke—surely anyone would seem an improvement?'

She laughed, a sound that Enno delighted to hear again. 'True.'

Tuoni brushed past, eager to make his report to his grandfather. 'Come on, Blue Man,' he called over his shoulder. 'Our chief will want to meet you.'

Freydis bit her lip, fighting the impulse to stop Blue Man going. Her father would not like a slave stepping out of place to be first in the introductions to the chief. He would blame her. But she had no illusions as to the amount of control she had over Blue Man: if he wanted to go, he would. Her dignity was best preserved by avoiding the clash of wills and taking her father's criticism on the chin.

'You can go if you wish,' she said.

A party of women were heading in her direction, intent on offering the jarl's daughter hospitality.

Enno nodded towards them. 'They'll look after you now,' he said brusquely, fearing he was showing too much tenderness around her.

'I'll manage, Blue Man.'

She watched him stalk away, his long narrow back held erect. He was attracting fascinated stares: the Sami did not seem afraid of him, but rather treated him like an exotic bird, blown off course during the spring migration, that had landed in their colony. They kept their distance but chattered excitedly among themselves. It reminded her that only her own people saw him as a slave first and foremost; here he was a man to be admired.

And she had to admit she was finding it almost impossible to think of him as a slave herself any longer; he had become much more than that to her.

'My lady, would you care to follow us?' a woman asked, gesturing towards one of the round tents pitched among the rocks. She had apple-red cheeks and fine lines around her eyes made by laughter.

'You are very kind,' Freydis replied. Just now the distance between her and the shelter looked impossible to cross. She had got around the ship by holding on to the side but now she had no support and her right leg was shaking, despite the splint under her skirt. Gritting her teeth, she took an experimental step towards the women but immediately crumpled to the ground. Humiliation burned hot in her chest.

'My lady, what ails you?' the woman asked anxiously, crouching at her side.

The pain rolled through Freydis; sweat beaded on her brow. 'My leg—I'm as unsteady as a two-legged stool.' She laughed self-mockingly—it was better than crying with frustration. 'If you would just give me a moment.'

The woman tutted when she spied the splint. 'No need. Come, we will carry you.'

'No, really—'

'I will not take no for an answer. You look as if you weigh no more than a sack of goose-down. Two of us can manage you with no problem.' She signalled to a second woman to assist her.

With a sigh, Freydis resigned herself to being carried across the camp clinging to their shoulders.

Tuoni led Enno through the mixed crowd of Sami and Norsemen gathered to listen to Tapiola and Ohthere as they sat together, sharing news and a meal. The jarl had been offered a bench while Tapiola squatted at his feet.

'Grandfather, look who I have brought to meet you!' Tuoni exclaimed excitedly.

Ohthere glanced up and frowned. ''Tis no one—my daughter's slave.' He took a savage bite of bread and chewed as if punishing it.

Tapiola, however, had risen to his feet, his dark eyes round with wonder. He stretched out a hand to touch Enno's arm warily. 'It is you. At last.'

Enno wondered what the old man meant. He caught Tuoni's eye, his brows raised in a question.

'What do you mean, Grandfather?' Tuoni

asked. He flicked his mane of dark hair back with a casual gesture as strands whipped across his face. 'Why "at last"?'

Tapiola smiled and pulled his grandson into his arms. 'You have brought a great blessing on to the tribe, my boy. I saw him in the smoke—the coming of the black wolf will restore many things to their right places.'

'Who's the black wolf?' asked Tuoni, but his eyes were already turned to Enno.

'Aye, that is him. His guardian came ahead and told of his arrival—the exile, the man alone. He makes a home for others but has none himself.'

'Bird crap,' muttered Ohthere rudely, taking a swig of mead. 'What you have there, Tapiola, is no blessing but a joke—a slave who won't work, won't serve without a fuss. My daughter can't control him, and I haven't the patience to try. If you like him so much, perhaps you should ask her to sell him to you.'

Tapiola politely inclined his head to Ohthere. 'My friend, you do not understand the man.'

'You're right about that,' snorted Ohthere.

'He has an unbent spirit. You cannot harness the wind; you won't be able to fetter this one.'

Ohthere's laugh had a cynical edge. 'But even the wind propels my ship for me. I have no desire to chain him. I'm a fair master—you know that. All I ask is loyalty and good service from those of my household.'

Tapiola nodded. 'That is true—and you are, as you say, a fair man—but the black wolf belongs to no household.'

Intrigued, Enno stood silently listening to the exchange. The old man appeared effortlessly to see into the heart of what he thought and felt about himself. In all his years of captivity, no northerner had ever understood what set him apart.

'Why do you call me Black Wolf? And how did you know I was coming?' Enno asked, breaking his silence as he placed his palm over Tapiola's fingers where they touched his forearm.

The old man stepped closer and raised his free hand to trace the swirls on Enno's cheeks. 'I have long known about you. I've seen you when I cross to the other world.'

The man's certainty made a chill shiver down Enno's spine. 'What are you? A . . . a warlock?' He moved out of reach, suspicious now that he was dealing with the dark powers.

'No, I am a . . . ' Tapiola searched for a word, 'one who sees.' He brushed his hand between them, as if moving aside a curtain. 'You need not fear me, Black Wolf. You are the dangerous one, not I.'

Alert to any threat to his tribe, Tuoni pushed between Tapiola and Enno, forcing his grandfather away from the stranger. 'He's dangerous? Why didn't you say at once! And I brought him here!'

Tapiola grinned, displaying a row of crooked teeth. 'You need not regret your actions, Tuoni. It is not we who have to fear him.'

Tuoni gazed wonderingly at the silent African. 'Then who?'

Tapiola looked into Enno's eyes. 'His enemies. Welcome.' He gestured to the rug. 'Will you eat with us?'

Ohthere rose to his feet as his slave took a place on the rug. 'If this is the company you choose, then I will see to my men. When do you expect the next reports from your scouts?'

Enno was impressed that Tapiola did not seem worried that he might have offended his guest of honour.

'Tonight,' said the chief. 'I will alert you the moment they arrive. Take your rest, Jarl. If I am not mistaken, you have not slept properly for many days.'

Ohthere muttered a reluctant agreement. 'How can I sleep when my son's life hangs in the balance?'

'But there is nothing you can do for the remainder of the day. I will send someone to your tent with a sleeping draught. You should feel no guilt making use of it. Your son needs you alert to be of any help to him and the other captives.'

Ohthere bowed, acknowledging that the man spoke the truth. 'Aye. And thank you. I knew I could count on you after our long years of association.'

With the Norseman gone, Tapiola's attention again riveted to Enno, his ancient face creased in an appreciative smile. 'So, traveller, tell me: where is the white wolf?'

Enno took a leisurely bite of the food, enjoying the rare sensation of being treated as a person of importance. 'Where's what?'

'The other warrior. When I see you, you are always the black wolf with the white.'

Enno shook his head. Perhaps the old man was a little crazy after all. Disillusionment spoiled his mood: it had been so heart-warming to be regarded as special for a few moments. 'I've got a white wolf?'

Tapiola nodded in complete seriousness.

'Sorry to disappoint you, sir, but I have no companion, wolf or human. As you said, I'm the man alone.'

'But White Wolf is alone too. Two strangers together—that's how you seem on the other side.'

'In that case, I've not met White Wolf yet.' Enno brushed crumbs from his lap. The conversation was making him uneasy. He didn't like to be reminded just how lonely he was—a man without family or even friends.

The old man was looking at him so intently that his gaze seemed to pass right through him, through skin, to the heart. 'You have met. You just don't know it yet.' With a gesture like a dog shaking water from its coat after a dip in a lake, Tapiola cast off his mood. 'Come, eat. Tuoni, sit down with us and tell me how you've fared these last few days.'

Freydis watched from her bed on a pile of sheepskins as Luonno, she of the apple cheeks, bustled around the tent to gather together the necessary items for her guest.

'Clean clothes,' the Sami woman said brightly, tapping a pile of bright blue cloth, 'new shoes,' she showed Freydis a pair of deerskin boots, 'and hot water for your wound.'

On cue, a second, younger woman, Luonno's sister, Paiva, entered the tent with a bowl. She had the same rosy cheeks and hair so blonde it was almost silver. 'We'll soon have you looking like the daughter of a jarl,' she said, placing the basin on the ground beside their guest.

The comment prompted Freydis to take a good look at herself. Over the last few days, her personal appearance had been the last of her considerations but she realized she was still wearing the torn blood-stained dress she had had on during the raid. Her hair was roughly plaited and far from clean. It was a wonder the women were not running away from her screaming.

'I'm sorry,' she said, waving to herself. 'There's been no time since—'

Luonno clucked understandingly. 'It's no wonder. A little thing like you with no one but those great clumsy men to nurse you. You need a mother's hand, child.' She helped Freydis out of her dress and threw it towards the tent-flap. 'Don't worry about that: Paiva will see if she can save it.' She said something rapidly in her own language and the younger woman left clutching a scrubbing board and the remains of Freydis's once fine gown.

As Freydis's own mother had died shortly after her birth, she had never known what it was like to have one care for her. *A little like this*, she mused, as Luonno gently washed every inch of her, murmuring sadly over scratches and bruises, exclaiming in distress when she finally unbound the wound and washed it with clean water. Her old nurse, Magda, had been of the school of tough love: no complaints allowed, a quick scrub in cold water and then a warning to keep out of trouble while she kept an eye on the far more challenging Toki.

Luonno replaced the splint, cushioning it with fleece.

'Here, put this on.' Luonno helped Freydis sit upright and pulled a padded tunic over her head. 'This will keep you warm.' She handed her a pair of thick woollen stockings. 'And these are for your feet.'

Freydis tried to reach down to put them on but the pain in her hip was too great. She flopped back on the skins, angry at being defeated by so simple a task, one that had once been as easy as breathing for her.

Luonno brushed the back of her hand over the girl's pale cheeks. 'Your injury causes you much suffering, yes?'

Freydis was going to deny it but the woman's gentle caress undermined her determination to appear strong before strangers. 'Yes. The bone's broken or cracked but I had to walk on it at the beginning. I think it's set badly.'

'Let me.' With a butterfly touch, Luonno rolled the stockings up to Freydis's knees and fastened them with a red garter. 'Warmer now?'

'Yes.'

'Then rest. I will ask our chief if he knows anything to help with your pain. He is a very wise man.'

'Thank you.'

As Freydis waited to fall asleep, she combed the sheepskin restlessly, wondering if Toki had anyone to help him deal with his pain.

11

The *Marauder* had rounded the North Cape and was now travelling east, parallel to the coast rumoured to be inhabited by the shape-shifting people called the Beormas. The sleek vessel cast a black shadow on the choppy grey waters, gliding like a cat sneaking up on its prey, dipping into bays to challenge the magicians to show themselves. Fighting sea-sickness in the heavy swell, Toki watched the lands pass—secretive fjords, mountains still white with snow, vast empty skies. To portside was nothing but ocean. The horizon was white—a line that might well be the very end of the world.

What would happen if you sailed that far? Toki wondered. Would you fall off the edge or get locked in everlasting ice? Maybe it led to Asgard of the gods, or the realm of giants and elves—the division that the gods could bridge with ease but humans never crossed. Wherever it led, he would still have to get away somehow and take his chances in this hostile land—either that or lose all honour.

Turning back to the ship, he saw his old nurse huddled in a ball not far from him. Magda's white hair hung in untidy ropes down her neck. None of them had had access to clean water for many days. Her nails were dirty and broken. It was particularly hard to see her reduced to this as she had always been a neat woman, hands scrubbed and clothes impeccable.

With a quick glance about him, Toki checked no one was watching him.

'Magda?' He shuffled towards her, his feet bound at the ankles, restricting his paces like a hobbled horse.

She looked up and fixed her tired eyes on him. 'Master Toki?'

'Yes, that's right.'

Tears began pouring down her cheeks as she rocked to and fro in distress. 'What have they done to you? My lovely boy, my lovely boy.'

Toki touched his swollen nose self-consciously. He probably looked worse than he felt. It was still hard to breathe but the pain was fading.

'I'm all right, really I am. But, Magda, why did you tell Kleppe about Freydis?'

He flinched inwardly when she gave him a dreamy smile. Her wits were half gone, Toki realized, she was escaping into memories.

'That little Elfling,' crooned Magda. 'I always had a soft spot for her, though I never let her know. She's tough, that one. She's her father's daughter all right, though he would never believe it. She looks like thistledown but will stick to life like a burr.'

He knelt beside her. 'Is that why you think she's still alive?' He gripped her hand. 'Or did you see her?'

Magda stroked his fingers and held his palm to her cheek. 'Such a kind boy.'

'Magda?'

'Should never have come to this.'

'Magda?'

She began to cry again. 'I didn't mean to tell that big man but I was in his way and he looked as if he was going to kill me, so . . . so I just blurted out that he shouldn't dare touch your old nurse. He was interested—forgot about killing me. Asked me all about the family. I'm sorry, so sorry.'

Toki shook his head. Her betrayal had happened as he feared: a bargain for her own life. He could hardly blame her. 'It doesn't matter. My sister was no secret, even if Father never spoke about her to outsiders.'

115

Recovering her focus, Magda's grip suddenly tightened, urgent now. She shoved him towards the side. 'You should go, Master Toki. They will kill you if you stay. Don't worry about us. They won't harm us; we're worth more to them alive than dead.'

'Hush now.' Toki tried to comfort her but she was frantic.

'I . . . I have something for you.' She fumbled in a pocket of her robe and pressed a knife into his palm. 'Remember how I used to take your toys when you deserved it?'

He nodded. Her fingers had indeed been quick and her beatings memorable.

'I took this off one of them.' She jerked her head at the pirates. 'They don't know yet, but when he misses it, he'll come looking. Hide it.'

He squeezed her fingers. 'Thank you.'

'Gods bless you, my boy.' She kissed his knuckles then pushed him away.

They had risked talking too long. Toki shuffled back to his crouching place, sliding the blade inside his tunic so that it fell down to his belt. He hunched over, praying that no one would notice the bulge. All he wanted now was an opportunity to use it. There was no point waiting for darkness for, at this time of year, it would never truly come.

In the end, it was Magda who provided Toki

with his chance. The crew had anchored in a bay for the night. After the evening meal, the pirates broke into small groups to entertain themselves. Some gathered around a board to bet on a game of counters; others stretched out to drink and joke. This was the time of day most feared by the captives, the time when eyes wandered and trouble was often found. Even harmless games could soon turn nasty.

One sailor got out a pipe and struck up a dance tune.

'Come on, girls, dance for us!' he called to the women.

They all avoided his eye—all except one. With a glance at Toki, Magda rose to her feet and began to sway and shuffle in time to the music, her ragged dress swishing around her swollen ankles.

'Surt's blood, that's disgusting!' laughed one onlooker. 'She's old enough to be my grandmother!'

The old nurse fluttered her eyelashes at the musician, a mockery of the seductive moves used by dancing girls. Pirates drifted over to watch the display, ridiculing Magda.

'Think anyone would fancy you, crone?' called one. 'I'd sooner kiss Kleppe!'

This comment brought a burst of laughter and calls for the big man to pucker up. Toki slid slowly backwards until his hips pressed against the rail.

The sailors may be ignoring him, but the other captives were watching his every move. A stout woman, a weaver by trade, gave Toki a nod of approval, straightened her spine and got up.

'Let me show you how it's danced where I come from,' she shouted lustily, pushing through the crowd. She snapped her fingers over her head and three other women followed, voices raised in crude challenges to the onlookers to match them step for step. Toki's heart pounded; his people were coming to his aid, creating a diversion for him. He owed it to them not to fail.

Turning to hide what he was doing, he eased the knife from his tunic and hacked at the ropes at his wrists. The position was awkward—he had to hold the knife backwards and could only achieve slight movement thanks to his immobilized hands but one by one the fibres gave way. Fingers tingled as the blood rushed back into them. He caught the rope before it could drop then crouched down to slash the binding on his ankles. With a glance over his shoulder to check that the pirates were still distracted playing with their latest prey, Toki straddled the side and let himself drop silently into the sea.

The cold took his breath away. Tucking the knife in his belt, he gasped and dived down, kicking for shore, every second expecting the alarm to be raised. The ship was moored only a bow's shot from land so Toki was able to clamber up the rocky beach before the cold water sapped all his energy. Taking great heaving breaths, he staggered behind a limpet-encrusted outcrop and risked a final look back at the ship. From the movement on deck, it appeared as if the dance was continuing, the women of Bjarkoy now partnering the sailors in a pretend display of high spirits. He prayed that their courage would not be rewarded with violent reprisals. But one thing was certain: he mustn't waste their sacrifice. Hurrying out of sight, he followed the path of a stream away from the beach.

The river led him into the welcome cover of a birch forest, sprawling southwards in a vast stone basin formed by the mountains. The salt of the sea gave way to the scent of the pollen shed by countless catkins that sprouted like tiny lambs' tails from the leafless branches. The air was alive with birdsong. Last year's leaves lay in a thick rotting blanket at his feet. He was freezing after his dip in the sea, but he had left with nothing but the knife.

'I'll get warm quick enough if I keep on moving,' he told himself. 'And too hot if Sulke catches me.'

The thought of what the pirates would do to him was like a whip at his heels. He pressed onwards with no clear aim but to get as far from the shore as he possibly could. He clung on to the hope that somehow his flight would enable him to help his people and return to Freydis. With every step he was aware that he was in all likelihood heading into even greater peril. This land belonged to the Beormas. He was surrounded by enemies no matter which direction he chose.

12

Waking in a warm nest of blankets, it took Freydis a moment to remember where she was. The Sami camp—she could see it through the tent-flap. The air was cool, barely warmed by the spring sunshine that had enticed the wild flowers into abundant display. The pasture that spread in the valley between the mountainsides was flush with tiny yellow blooms like gilding on a king's shield. It felt like a place apart from the violence and death inflicted by the raiders down at sea level.

Emerging a few more steps from sleep, her stomach reminded her that she needed to visit the privy. Rolling out of her covers, she groped around for the crutch Blue Man had brought her the night before. He'd entered the tent close to midnight and dropped it by her side without a word of explanation; she suspected he had made it himself as the handle was whittled beautifully smooth. She stroked it, smiling at the unpredictable behaviour of her slave-who-was-not-a-slave. After briefly experimenting and finding the crutch could hold her weight, Freydis hobbled out of her tent, leaving the other women still sleeping.

On her return to the tent, she spotted Blue Man standing on the lip of the valley, much as he had done on arrival, his tall figure silhouetted against the sky. It wasn't hard to see what had caught his attention. With the sun at his back, the west was glowering under a slate-grey cloud slashed by a vivid double rainbow. She couldn't help herself—she *wanted* to be with him whatever his mercurial mood this morning.

'That's Bifrost—the bridge to the home of the gods,' Freydis said, hopping up behind him. Deftly, she swung herself to sit on a rock, pleased to have an opportunity to show him that she was getting the hang of the crutch. 'If you jump on that, you can slide all the way to Asgard—but the trick is in catching up with it.'

'Oh yes?' Enno pulled his gaze from the horizon to look down at her. 'And how do you know?'

She waved her hand at the rainbow. 'I've chased it, of course. You can't ever reach the end before it moves off—the gods are too clever for us.'

Enno shaded his eyes. 'It looks easy enough: take a boat and sail to that island there.'

'You could—but it will escape you. It's impossible to trap.'

'And what would I do in Asgard anyway?' He sat down on a stone beside her, waiting for her suggestions. 'You're the skald—you tell me.' He was teasing her.

'Hardly a skald—I just like music.'

'I've heard you. You're better than many a skald I've come across.'

'Why, thank you—I think.' She wrinkled her nose. 'Just how many skalds have you met?'

He smiled: she wasn't accepting the compliment easily. 'Enough. Now go on: tell me what I could do in the home of your gods.'

Freydis shrugged. 'You could find out your future from the Norns at the Well of Urd?'

Remembering Tapiola's prediction that he may never return home, Enno wasn't sure that he wanted the Vikings' goddesses of destiny to tell him anything. Not that he believed in them.

'No thanks. What else?'

Freydis warmed to her task. 'Tickle Jormungand, the serpent that circles our world?'

'And cause an earthquake? Not likely.'

'Ah no—earthquakes are Loki shivering as

123

poison drips on his face—his punishment for killing the god Balder.'

'Bloodthirsty lot, your gods, aren't they?' Enno was tempted to kiss the earnest look off her face as she told him these tales, but then he recalled that he had vowed never to show any affection for a Viking.

'I suppose they are. What other kind of gods are there?'

He threaded his fingers together, holding them cupped in his lap, the stance he took when praying. 'I believe in one God, maker of everything.'

Freydis gave him an incredulous look. 'Just the one?'

'Just one.'

'But wouldn't he be too busy to hear our petitions? How does he manage with so much to do?'

Enno was amused that her first thought was concern for the overworked deity. 'I imagine he's got it under control.'

Freydis chewed her bottom lip. Enno reminded himself that he was absolutely not going to kiss her. Her father would kill him for a start. 'No, no, I don't think I can believe in that. The world is too big for one god on his own. And what about a wife? Does he have a wife?'

'He's a bit above wives and such things. That's for us humans.'

'Why?'

'It just is.'

Freydis fiddled with the talisman around her neck. Blue Man's faith was very simple, but extraordinary. She couldn't imagine a world without the gods and goddesses who controlled the harvests, the sea, the rising and setting of the sun. Still, if that was what he wanted to think, that was his business. 'I was right: Toki would love meeting you. He was always fascinated by new things.'

'Seems to me that you are too.'

'Am I?' Freydis's face broke into a smile as the realization struck. 'I am, aren't I? I'm like Toki.'

'He sounds like a fine brother.'

'The best.'

They sat a while longer in companionable silence, watching the rainbow. Enno stole sidelong glances at her pensive profile, wondering what he was going to do about his feelings for his Viking mistress. They made him shamefully soft-hearted when it came to anything involving her.

'Uh-oh, here comes trouble.' Freydis nudged Enno, nodding in the direction of Tuoni striding towards them.

'Trouble?'

'Don't say you haven't noticed?' Freydis rolled her eyes. 'Every girl in this tribe has him lined up as their target. He moved through them last night at the meal like a prince in his court, flicking that long hair of his, posing to make sure they all caught his best side.'

Enno grinned, assessing the youth as he approached. 'Doesn't seem that he has a bad side. He's almost as handsome as me.'

'And he knows it.' Freydis curled her lip in disgust.

Enno was secretly pleased she hadn't denied she considered both of them handsome. 'Don't you like him?'

'He's all right, I suppose.' Freydis was reluctant to admit that she was immune to the boy's soulful dark eyes and good looks because she was already daydreaming about a certain African warrior. She had picked over every conversation she had had with Blue Man, looking for the least sign that he felt any affection for her. So far she'd found little cause for hope.

'He is the tribe's favoured son, being Tapiola's grandchild.'

'I know that. I'm not stupid.'

'No, but you sound a little jealous.'

She gave a hollow laugh. 'You're wrong. How

126

could I be jealous of that?' She flicked her wrist in a twirling gesture to encompass everything about the Sami boy.

'Good morning, Blue Man!' called Tuoni.

'Morning.' Enno tapped the ground beside them. 'Join us?'

'Thank you.' Tuoni threw himself into a long-legged sprawl, making the grass look like a king's couch. Freydis wondered when he would notice her presence.

'Good morning, Tuoni,' she said pointedly.

He muttered something in reply.

'Did you sleep well?'

'Fine. Look . . . um . . . Freydis, do you mind if I have a word with Blue Man? Alone.'

She did mind. 'I see.' Using the crutch to steady herself, she swung herself away, eating up the ground with each angry pace.

Enno watched her go, his brow creased. 'Why did you do that?' he asked Tuoni.

'Do what?' Tuoni asked airily.

'Ignore her, then send her away.'

The boy shrugged.

Enno felt his anger rise. 'She's had enough people making her feel worthless. It's hard to believe in yourself when others tell you you are nothing.' He should know: he'd had many years of it.

'I didn't tell her she was nothing!' protested Tuoni, sitting up indignantly.

'You did—by your actions.'

'Sorry.' He threw a bit of grass over the ledge, not sounding the least bit apologetic.

'Why treat her that way?'

'She's that man's daughter. I hate all Vikings on principle.'

There was something in the boy's petulance that reminded Enno uncomfortably of his own vow not to care for any Norseman. 'Your grandfather doesn't.'

'My grandfather has to be careful. I don't think he likes Ohthere much either. And I know you don't.'

'And what has that to do with his daughter?'

Tuoni scowled. 'Look, Blue Man, I didn't come to talk about them. You worry about her too much. A daughter of a jarl could never feel worthless, not with all of us running around after her.'

'I didn't see you doing much running.' His arguments making no impact, Enno decided to change tack and appeal to Tuoni's vanity. 'She likes you, you know.'

Tuoni pricked up his ears. 'Really?'

Enno hid his smile. 'Yes. She'll be the last person to admit it to you, but she thinks you're handsome.'

128

Tuoni unconsciously swiped the hair back off his forehead. 'You think?'

'I know. She told me. So you be nice to her.'

Tuoni was flattered enough to be magnanimous. 'I'll be careful.'

'Good. Now, what did you want to ask me?'

Annoyed that Tuoni had spoiled her private moment with Blue Man, Freydis hurried away with as much speed as she could manage.

'Puffed-up billy goat,' she fumed. 'Conceited oaf.'

'Hey, Freydis, where are you off to?' Leif jogged to catch up with her.

'Oh, sorry, Leif.' She wiped her damp brow with the back of her hand, leaving a smudge. 'I was in a bit of a mood—not fit company for people—so I was going to visit the herd up the valley.'

'May I come with you?'

Freydis nodded. She had always had a soft spot for her father's second-in-command. 'If you want to live dangerously.'

He chuckled and fell into step with her.

'You're managing well with the crutch.'

'Not too bad, now I've given up putting any weight on my stupid leg.'

'All of us are really sorry for what you went through.'

She said nothing. It was not a subject she could discuss with anyone yet.

Leif held back a bramble to allow her past unhindered. 'How are you getting on with your new slave?'

'Ah.' She cleared her throat in embarrassment, strangely annoyed to hear Leif referring to him in that dismissive manner. There was no way that she was going to tell Leif that she was falling a little in love with her proud Blue Man.

'Like that, is it? Do you want me to have words with him?'

'No! We get along fine. He's quite kind really.'

'Kind? Slaves aren't there to be kind; they're supposed to serve.'

The meadow was no distance from the camp and they soon reached the herd. The reindeer drifted over the pasture, nose to ground, nudging at the new grass, tough lips rooting it out of crevices in lichen-covered rocks.

'The Sami are very generous to us, aren't they?' said Freydis, deciding on a change of subject as they turned back to the camp.

Leif steadied her over an uneven section of the path. 'You like them?'

'Who wouldn't?'

'That's good. Very good. You see, Freydis, I sought you out for a reason. I thought someone should tell you before your father . . . well, anyway, we had word from the scouts last night. Sulke's gone north, heading towards the land of the Beormas. We're setting out in pursuit today.'

'So soon?' Freydis dreaded the humiliation of being carried back down the cliff path again but she didn't think she'd quite mastered the crutch enough to do it alone. 'We must get back quickly so I can be ready.'

He placed his work-roughened hand on her forearm. 'Ah, you see, the thing is, your father's decided you should stay here.'

'Stay?'

'It's too dangerous to take you with us.'

'But what if you don't come back this way?' She refused to consider the possibility that they might not live long enough to return. 'I . . . I can't stay here.'

'The chief has said you'll be very welcome. Blue Man will remain behind to make sure all your needs are met.'

She wasn't listening. Her father was going to abandon her again. First she'd lost Toki, then her home, now her own people.

131

'No, no please, Leif. Send me back to Bjarkoy—or take me with you. I don't belong here.'

Leif gave her a reproving look. 'It's just as well that I told you myself. You know that these pleas would not have gone down well with your father.'

'But, Leif!'

'You have no choice, Elfling. These are good people. They'll look after you.'

Her real fear was that once he left, her father would forget her and never come back.

'I don't care. You can't leave me here. I want to go with you.'

Leif took her shoulders and gave her a little shake, reading the panic in her face. 'Stop it, Freydis. You are the jarl's daughter. You know your duty and that is to obey your father.'

She let her head drop forward and screwed her eyes closed. 'He just wants to get rid of me. He won't come back, will he?'

Leif had heard the rumours of what had gone wrong between Ohthere and Freydis so knew she was right to worry. 'I won't let him forget.' He tapped her nose. 'And when we get Toki back, you can bet that your brother won't waste a day before rushing to fetch you.'

'Toki.' The soft word sounded more like a prayer.

'That's right. Now cheer up, my lady, and show your father that you have steel in your backbone. He'll respect you more for accepting his will without a fuss.'

'No, he won't.'

He chucked her under the chin. 'Well, the rest of us then. We'll want our singer back. Who else will entertain us on the *Sea Otter* while you are here?'

Freydis understood that Leif was only trying to help. It wasn't his fault. 'You'll have to get Sigtrygger to tell you one of his stories.'

Leif groaned—as Freydis knew he would. 'Spare us! Anything but that!'

By the time they reached camp, Freydis had almost got control of her emotions. She could do nothing to change her father's resolve and any fuss she made would meet with a smart reproof. All that was left to her was to retain her dignity and pretend she didn't mind.

The Vikings were ready to depart, waiting only on Leif to return. Ohthere strode out of Tapiola's tent as soon as they appeared.

'What kept you?' he asked impatiently.

'I had something I had to do,' Leif replied evasively.

Ohthere was in too much of a hurry to question him. 'Let's go. We can't afford to lose any more time this morning.' He turned to his daughter standing quietly in Leif's shadow. 'Freydis, you'll be staying here.'

She met his gaze, her clear eyes a challenge. 'Yes, Papa.'

He frowned, surprised by her lack of reaction. 'Be good. Don't get in anyone's way.'

'I won't.'

'Well then.' He paused for a moment, then took a step towards her, mindful that they had an audience for their farewell. 'Come, bid me goodbye then.' He held out his arms in an uncertain gesture, like a trainer facing a skittish horse.

Freydis stood her ground. She wasn't going to pretend a show of affection when she knew there was nothing behind it on his part. 'Goodbye, Papa.'

Her subdued dignity stirred something in Ohthere. He crossed the distance between them and gave her a brief hug. 'We'll come back when we can,' he promised gruffly.

'Of course.' Freydis clamped her lips together to stop the pleas that were clamouring to spill out. It wasn't fair that he showed her kindness now—it was easier to bear his dislike of her when it was constant.

Ohthere released her and faced his men. 'Right, then. Move out!'

Freydis watched the crew of the *Sea Otter* file

quickly away, disappearing over the lip of the valley for the steep climb down. From her experience of the last few weeks, it was hard not to believe that this might be the last time she would see any of them. From being a girl who had never strayed far from home, she was now a stranger in a foreign land, among people she did not know and who had scant reason to care for her with no Ohthere on hand to impress. And to look after her, she had a slave who was no slave; a man whom she couldn't help wanting, against all that was expected of her as a jarl's daughter.

'Welcome to my new life,' Freydis murmured before turning to go back to her tent.

13

Early spring was not a good time to scavenge from the land: too early for fruits, too late for nuts. Though weak with hunger, Toki did not dare turn aside to hunt. It would take time to make snares and traps for the small creatures of the forest and he told himself that it was better to stumble on with an empty belly than be recaptured with a full one.

As Toki made his way down the valley, the land did not narrow and climb, but remained fairly level. This gave him hope that his luck had changed for the better and he had struck the course of one of the longer rivers of this country that wound its way through the mountains. But where there was a river-valley, he guessed that there would also be people; with so little cultivatable earth this far north, such places were usually highly prized and fiercely defended. The land of the Beormas was an empty country, rocks more plentiful than trees, a place that made him long for the pastures of his own island home.

Toki stumbled on with bleeding feet, alert for any sign of trouble. He knew that his only hope of survival lay in remaining undetected.

He came across his first settlement near night-fall: a ring of tents, up-ended sledges on a rack waiting for the next snows, a paddock holding a tough-looking horse and two domesticated reindeer, a small boat beached on the river bank by the boat-house. He judged it was a semi-permanent base, possibly the winter quarters of the nomadic Beormas. It was too much to ask that it be empty—not with the stock in residence, but if most of the tribesmen were away on their spring tasks of round-ing up the wild reindeer, fishing and hunting, he might be able to steal some food and slip by without being noticed.

Or could he ask for help?

Toki considered this for a few minutes, weigh-ing what he'd heard about these people against his perilous situation. Sulke would hunt him down. Alone, without supplies, in an unfamiliar land, Toki's chance of evading his foe was slight.

But the Beormas were shape-changers. Enemies of all Norsemen.

With a groan of regret, Toki decided he could not risk it. A quick raid on any unguarded supplies and then he had to be out of here.

Using the grey shadows of night to hide his presence, he crept towards the tents. As he feared, there were people inside one of them: he could see the flicker of a fire and the smoke curling out of the hole in the centre of the tent-roof. Laughter and the smell of food cooking—both made him feel hungry for a meal and companionship. On Bjarkoy, he'd taken such things for granted; now they seemed more precious to him than any number of gold rings or silver brooches. He took some slow breaths to steady his pounding heart, surveying the land around him. Two eider ducks slept with heads tucked under wings on the river bank near the boat—little did they know, but they had just volunteered to become supper. Silently, Toki approached, then swooped down and made a grab for the drake. With a skilled move, he broke its neck before it had time to make a noise. Not so the female: she raised the alarm, quacking with terror as Toki took off. In a few seconds, the night went from calm to noisy confusion. A man rushed out of the nearest tent, shouting something in his own language, then set off in pursuit with a spear clenched in his fist. Risking a glance over his shoulder, Toki saw two others—young boys—join the man; they cursed the thief and brandished weapons. Toki dived for cover, hoping they had not seen him, but he was well aware that any tracker worth his salt would be able to pick up the signs of his hurried flight for the trees.

The body of the drake hung heavy in his hand as Toki loped further into the forest. He did not like stealing from people who had so little. And now, before the duck could be of any use to him, he would have to find a place where it was safe to pluck and cook it. He would swap it for a loaf of stale bread in a heartbeat.

Chest heaving, sweat dripping in his eyes, Toki paused in the shelter of an old pine tree, its trunk split and only half the branches still bearing green needles. He strained his ears for the sound of people on his trail. He could hear nothing—but that did not mean they were not there. A good huntsman was trained to creep up on prey. Toki moved slowly now, choosing quiet over speed. In the Beormas' shoes, he would spread out, hoping to net the thief between them in a sweep through the forest. If he was careful enough, he should be able to double back and slip past them. The boat on the river bank was too much of a temptation to be ignored. He had realized too late that he should have gone for that rather than answered the demands of his stomach.

Suddenly, the ground beneath his feet gave way, branches snapped, earth showered him as he plunged into a bear pit. A horrid vision of sharpened stakes flashed through his mind. He landed heavily, stunned—but in one piece.

'Black Surt!' Toki swore, spitting out sticks and leaves, wiping the dust from his eyes. Fortune had favoured him to the extent that he had stumbled into a trap to catch live animals—though why anyone would want a bear to be still breathing when they checked their snare was beyond him. Toki got shakily to his feet and patted the walls—just earth. It should not be too difficult to climb out with the help of his dagger and a stout stick to act as handholds. He had to be quick before the Beormas caught up with him.

Hitching the drake to his belt, he stabbed the wall with the knife. It held. He looked up. Only ten feet to go.

After a climb that tested his muscles to the limit, he reached the last pull with his left arm and was able to plant the knife in level ground with his right. Immediately, a boot stepped on his fist and a hand grabbed the back of his tunic, hauling him out.

'Let go of the knife!' warned the Beorma man, pricking Toki between the shoulder blades with his spear.

Someone else tugged the drake from his waistband and muttered a few derogatory words in his own language—the voice youthful. One of the boys, Toki guessed.

The pressure of the boot increased on his fingers. 'Let go, Viking!'

Toki opened his hand, waiting for the moment when the man would take his foot off him to retrieve the knife. The crush of leather on flesh eased. Toki rolled from under the spear, making a grab for the dagger hilt as he moved, cannoning into the man's legs and bringing him down as he slid free. Before Toki could spring up, one of the boys charged him—but he had expected that. He planted his foot in his assailant's stomach and threw him over his head. Toki surged to his feet, alert for the third one, only to see him backing away, his scant five feet no match for the young, hungry Viking. Noting the weak link in the hunting party and the short axe in the boy's hand, Toki went right for him, intent on gaining a weapon and getting a hostage.

'No!' shouted the man behind him, but too late. Toki grabbed the axe, wrested it easily from the

141

child's grip with minimal struggle, and backed him to a tree, knife pointing to his throat.

Silence fell in the clearing around the bear trap, save the heavy breathing of all four combatants and the whimper of terror from the little Beorma hostage. Toki's brain was whirling, trying to think how best to turn this situation to his advantage.

'I mean you no harm!' he said, though the fact that he had a blade at the boy's throat rather undermined his attempt to convince them he had peaceful intentions. 'I just want some supplies and a way out of here.' He heard movement behind him. 'Stay back!' He shoved the axe haft into his belt and hooked the boy around the middle, swinging round so that now Toki had his back to the tree and his hostage in front. The two Beormas stopped in their tracks and Toki got his first look at their faces. The older man had a bald pate with long hair at the sides hanging to his shoulders. A thick dark-brown beard was divided into two forks on his broad chest. His face was flatter than a Norseman, eyes slanted by a smooth upper lid, but he dressed much like Tapiola's people in the padded jacket and trousers of this region. The boy had the same almond eyes and dead-straight black hair cropped at his ears in a bowl-shaped cut. His expression was ugly, full of bitter anger at the stranger who had bested them—for the moment.

'Give me what I ask and I'll let the little one go,' Toki continued.

With a sudden gust of courage, the hostage surprised him by stamping on his instep, trying to squirm free.

'Stop that!' he growled, hefting the boy off his feet and squeezing him tightly around the middle. 'I don't want to hurt you.'

The man barked a command and the boy went limp. The elder held up a hand, palm open in a plea. 'Let her go.'

Her? Toki took a quick confused glance downwards and now took in the long black plaits and small frame of his armful. The leggings had confused him but the man spoke the truth: he was holding a girl. But Toki knew he couldn't afford to be so gallant as to give up his one advantage.

'I won't harm her if you do as I ask. You have to understand: I took the duck because I was hungry and had no choice. I bear no ill-will to you and yours. I need help.'

The girl may have stopped struggling but her tongue now took up the battle. 'Stinking, thieving Viking!'

'Guilty on all counts,' admitted Toki, impressed by her bravery.

'I hope you rot in Surma's gullet. Kill him, Father. Don't worry about me.'

'Aino!' the man exclaimed.

'Do it!'

Toki increased the pressure around the girl's waist so she had to gasp for breath. 'Hush now, little Valkyrie, your father and I are negotiating.' He studied the man before him, trying to gauge his mood. 'Will you help me?'

The boy took a step forward. 'Let my sister go, you demon!'

The man jerked him back by the back of his jacket. 'Quiet, Lempo. What kind of man threatens a girl, Viking?'

Toki was not proud of himself. 'A desperate one. I won't harm a hair on her head if you would just swear that you will help me.'

The man narrowed his eyes. Then he shrugged. 'I choose not to aid you. Do your worst!'

The man had called his bluff.

'Father!' exclaimed the two youngsters in shock.

'You'd prefer her dead than to give a stranger food?' Toki asked incredulously.

'Yes.' The man waved his hand at his daughter.

'Go on. Do what you have to do.' The Beorma father turned his eyes briefly to the girl, his expression a subtle request for her to trust him. She immediately went still.

Toki felt sick. He'd never intended to injure anyone—he didn't have it in him to punish the innocent. His ploy had failed.

'Curse you!' he grunted, pushing the girl from him and pulling the axe from his belt, ready to defend himself against the inevitable attack. At full strength he would not have doubted that he could take both Beormas, but now, with black dots of exhaustion humming across his vision, he knew he was in no fit state to win. Better death in battle though, than life as Sulke's slave.

'Easy, lad,' the man said, hugging his daughter and putting her behind him. 'Viking, I'm not going to fight you. I believe you now.'

'Believe me?' Wearily, Toki wiped his brow, still not ready to drop his guard.

'You proved you would not hurt us. I did not think you would.'

'Thanks for telling me, Papa,' muttered Aino.

'You know I wouldn't risk you, sweetheart,' her father said with a smile as she struggled to hold on to her annoyance. 'The only one who need die this night is the duck the boy stole.' He prodded the carcass with the toe of his boot. 'Let us not waste it.'

Toki swayed. 'You're going to help me? A Viking? You're not going to turn into bears or something and eat me?'

The man snorted. 'Is that what you've heard? I suppose we could. Aino, Lempo, what do you think?'

The two youngsters, twins by the look of their matching scowls, bared their teeth at Toki.

'Too much bother,' the girl said stiffly, her dignity ruffled by having been captured.

'Aye, I'll not waste our magic on him,' spat Lempo.

'Well then, that's settled. Let us return home and see if we can find the stranger some food. It seems that he's already killed the meat for us.' He stooped to pick up the duck, deliberately turning his back on Toki to show that he no longer feared him.

Warily, Toki offered the girl the axe. She snatched it from his hand with a sniff. Following in the footsteps of the three Beormas, Toki began to question if the rumours about shape-changing might have been somewhat exaggerated.

'I would be grateful for a roof over my head—just for the night,' he assured the Beorma man, but then remembered Sulke. 'I should warn you: there's someone hunting me. He's very dangerous—ruthless.'

'Don't worry about that,' the man said, giving a dismissive wave of his hand. 'We'll just turn into bears and chase them off, won't we?'

His son and daughter laughed.

Toki shook his head. They had no idea who they were dealing with.

WOLF CRY

'Through my lips I stirred
from the depths of my heart
Odin's sea of verse
about the craftsman of war.'

(EGIL'S SAGA)

14

Enno was delighted when Ohthere decided to leave him behind to guard Freydis. He had got his wish to be with her without the other Vikings around, in a place where he felt strangely at home. The Sami accepted his difference once the initial shock had worn off and made no great fuss about his skin colour or distant origins. They were more interested in Tapiola's claim that Enno was Black Wolf—whatever that meant—and treated him with great respect.

It was like sunshine after a long winter to feel a proper man again, not a slave.

And that was exactly how he acted. He was grateful that Freydis did not challenge him on his behaviour as he did not want to force the conversation as to who was in charge in their relationship. He let his actions speak for themselves. He did not consult her as to what he would do each day, but took off with the herdsmen or hunters as the whim took him. In the evenings, he sat with the men, swapping stories, telling jokes, listening to the youngsters boast. He kept himself closely informed as to Freydis's welfare, thanks to the women who looked after her, but he tried to maintain a distance so that no damaging reports would filter back to her father of any inappropriate conduct between them, limiting his time with her so that he would not betray his feelings.

After a week at the camp, half the men left with the herd to resume the spring grazing on the island of Soroy. Chief Tapiola had decided that the threat of Sulke had passed for the moment but he chose to keep the rest of the tribe safely hidden in their stronghold in case Sulke came back spoiling for revenge. The pirates would not be able to march in next time and claim tribute. Word had gone out to the friendly tribes. If Sulke wanted anything from one of the Sami tribes—Finna, Beorma, or Terfinna—he would have to fight. The Sami men went prepared to ambush any pirates who tried to land on Soroy.

Tuoni was among those who remained with the women in the stronghold. The boy did not take the decision kindly, protesting to his grandfather that he wanted to go with the fighters and punish any raiders who dared land on their pastures.

'Exactly why he should stay here,' Tapiola confided to Enno late one night while they watched the central fire burn down to embers, tankards of weak mead in hand. The interior of the chieftain's tent was decorated with line-paintings of the animals they hunted: deer, seal, wolf, and bear. In the flickering light, they came alive, swarming across the pale brown fields of the roof. 'Besides, I would like him to stay with me while we prepare our defence. It will be good for him to see that being a leader is not all about fighting, but about planning and talking.'

'He's a good lad,' murmured Enno. Running a hand over his eyes, he wondered what spell he was under, seeing creatures move when he knew they were but drawings. Had he had too much to drink?

'Yes, but he's impetuous.'

'And you weren't at his age?'

Tapiola chuckled. 'And how is your little mistress?'

Enno shrugged off his instinctive annoyance at the title. 'The jarl's daughter? She's well, I think. I've not seen her today.'

'Ah.' The old man waited a beat. 'She intrigues me, that one.'

'How so?'

153

'On the surface, she seems so cheerful. The women like her. Always smiling, never asking for anything, getting on with things despite the trouble she has with walking, and yet . . . '

'And yet?'

Tapiola threw a clod of peat on the dying fire. 'You do not get to my age without learning a little about people. There's much more beneath the surface of that one. I'd like to test her.'

Enno was suddenly alert. He would not let anyone harm Freydis. 'What do you mean?'

'Nothing bad, I assure you, my friend. I'd like to test you too.'

'What is this testing?'

'It's our way—how we find out who we really are. I know a lot about you already but there's more you need to understand and you'll only discover what this is when you undergo the test.'

Enno remained silent. He was not sure what he felt about his host's insights into people. It was unsettling.

'If you'd been brought up amongst us, you would have already been through it. And it looks as if she might be here some time.' Tapiola picked up a charred stick and idly drew a four-footed animal on a flat white stone. 'Perhaps if she went through our test she might feel as if she belonged. It would help her, I think, as she does not trust our welcome.'

'And me?'

'Ah, Blue Man,' Tapiola flourished the stick at him like a wand, 'you hold so much back from us, even your true name. Will you ever belong anywhere again? You see yourself clearly but not your destiny. You have an illusion—a memory of home—but could you really return even if you had the chance?' He threw the stick on to the embers; it flared briefly then succumbed to the flames. 'The test will not hurt; it makes us part of each other as it is an experience we share; it defines our tribe. Perhaps it will do the same for you if you let it.'

Enno was silent for a moment. The old man saw too well; the chief had sensed the hunger in him to be part of a family again, an urge which warred with his desire to return to Africa where he had no one left. He'd even found himself wondering what kind of wife Freydis would make him, even though he knew this was an impossible dream. Maybe, if he did this thing, he would emerge more at peace with himself; that had to be worth the risk. 'I'll undertake the test and, if it does me no harm, then I will allow you to ask Freydis if she wants to do it too.'

'Gatekeeper to the mistress you do not even

acknowledge, Blue Man?' Tapiola's lined face wrinkled with humour.

Enno winced and took a gulp of mead to disguise his discomfort.

'It is all right: you do not have to hide from me that you care for the little one even if you pretend otherwise.'

'I do not care for her.'

'Of course you don't.'

'I merely offer her my protection as I am duty bound, a man of honour to someone weaker than him.'

'I understand.'

Enno let the matter lapse, aware he was getting the worst of the argument.

'All right, Chief, what do I have to do to take this test of yours?'

Tapiola brushed his hands together, wiping off the blue-black stain of charcoal. 'I'll fetch you at daybreak. Make sure you have a good rest tonight. You'll need your wits about you tomorrow.'

Tapiola led Enno further up the valley than he had yet gone in his explorations, beyond the small pasture, through the thickets of willow scrub, to the bottom of a rock scree that spilled over the mountainside like a stone fleece sheared off some giant ram of legend. It was a cold, damp day, grey clouds grazing the top of the mountainsides and dumping their burden on the barren rocks below— just the kind of northern weather Enno hated, making him pine for blue skies and African sun.

The old man halted and pointed up the slope.

'You must go on your own from here.'

'Go where?'

'You see that pile of larger rocks there?'

Enno nodded from under his reindeer hide hood, raindrops dripping from the brim like a diamond fringe.

'Climb up to them and then go in.' Tapiola handed him a waterskin.

'Go in where?'

'You'll see.'

'And do what?'

'You'll find out.' Tapiola turned away. 'Drink the water. I'll be down the path near the spring,' he called over his shoulder. 'Come and find me when you've finished.'

Muttering a stream of good humoured curses against evasive old men and their ideas of help, Enno began the difficult climb up to the rocks, taking frequent sips of the bitter-tasting liquid.

'He's put something in it,' Enno murmured,

wiping a drip off his chin. It wasn't unpleasant exactly, just odd, making his tongue tingle.

Soon he had little attention to spare for the drink: the scree was unstable, giving way under his feet so that he had to use his hands to stop sliding all the way to the bottom. He was thankful he had accepted the Sami people's gift of leather boots as well as the reindeer cloak.

Freydis will never manage this, Enno found himself thinking.

He'd have to stop worrying about her, he chided himself. He should never have grown attached to her. Tapiola's tribe were good people; she was in gentle hands; there was nothing to stop him leaving. He'd check that this test was safe, wait to see how she did, then say his farewells. Yes, that was best. It was time to move on.

Only he knew that he wouldn't.

At the expense of some skinned knuckles, he reached the pile of stones Tapiola had pointed out. Close to, they were much bigger than he expected, huge slabs split from the mountain, stacked on each other so that only a narrow entrance was left at their base.

Entrance to what? Enno wondered. He guessed that he had to find out for himself.

Being tall, it was a squeeze to fit inside. He

debated if he should go feet or head first. Peering into the darkness, he did not relish either prospect. Head first, he decided, and on his back.

Using his feet to propel himself forward, he shuffled into the narrow gap. He found it a horrible sensation, like burying oneself alive. Soon only his feet were left outside, the rest of him swallowed up in the hole, all light blocked by his own body. He lay there for a moment, wondering what to do next. There was no more room to go on; his head was up against rock.

Was this it? The test? See if you could squeeze yourself into this slot in the earth? It seemed an anti-climax after all the other possibilities he had been imagining.

I'll give it a few minutes, he told himself, *then shuffle out and tell Tapiola I did it. That would have to satisfy him.*

Eyes staring at nothing, Enno let the darkness enfold him.

Not a tomb, more like a womb, he thought.

His heart rate slowed, recovering from the climb. The rock no longer seemed to press on him, but held him up, sustaining him. The buzz left by the drink faded, leaving a dreamy sensation behind. Not quite drunk, but not quite normal either.

Enno's thoughts wandered, gliding through

the darkness like bats to their cave, finding their way home.

I'm a child of God's earth. Made from dust and breath in a garden, brought out of paradise to this cold exile, my fall from God's favour. So unfair.

So unfair.

I'm angry, Enno realized, eyes glaring at blank stone, *angry with my Creator.*

The mood bubbled and built. *Why me? Why was I marked out to be taken prisoner that day?* He wanted to howl with grief and loss, bite, run, anything to punish the One that had sent him here.

What did I do to deserve this? Nothing.

Enno closed his eyes, breathing hard to control his emotions.

I have never let myself grieve, he thought, *only allowed myself to feel anger. There is so much of it inside me that it is like molten rock tossed from a volcano that over time cools and turns to stone. I carry a heavy lump of the stuff with me at all times. I think that is my true fetter.*

But there was no way to punish God for this slavery of the soul—the very idea was ludicrous. And wrong. It went against everything Enno knew about His justice and goodness.

Enno blinked. As he lay raging against his fate, shapes started to appear on the ceiling above him,

160

faint white lines glowing against black rock. He reached his hand up to touch and felt the scratching on the smooth surface. The marks became clearer, taking the shape of creatures like those in Tapiola's tent. Closest to his face was the fluid form of a wolf running, led by its sharp nose and with its tail arrowing out behind. Enno felt his anger drain away, replaced by curiosity.

Where are you off to, my friend? He brushed his fingertips over the painting. *Fleeing pursuit or on the scent of prey?*

Further to his right emerged the outline of a deer, head curved to look over its shoulder at the wolf.

Is that your quarry? wondered Enno.

To the left, a hand's breadth from the wolf's tail, a party of humans followed, stick-like weapons raised over heads. Enno could almost hear the shouts and jeers of the hunters.

Then something shifted. He no longer imagined the voices: they were real—harsh, excited, lusting for blood.

He had to flee.

Hide.

The deer he hunted bounded out of sight but he was too busy saving himself to worry about the loss. He could not afford to stop. Far from his den, the only safety was in flight. Tongue lolling in his open mouth, claws skittering over uneven ground, tail whipping up and down—

Arrows fell, a spear flew past him.

No pack, no home, no mate—not unless he turned and fought for them.

But he didn't turn, couldn't take the risk. He ran on until the arrow hit him between the shoulder blades, bringing him to the ground. Black Wolf yelped, sight dimming as the wound overpowered him.

When Enno came to, he found stones digging into his back, his muscles cramped from lying so long on the ground, his body bathed in cold sweat. With a groan, he shuffled out of the hole, using his heels and hands to lever himself along. When daylight hit his face, he closed his eyes against the pain.

What had happened in there? He felt as if he'd died when the arrow struck but he was here, still breathing, still alive.

He rolled over on to his stomach and curled into a ball. His head was pounding. If Tapiola had sent him on the dream-trip with his herbs, Enno did not like the return journey. His throat was dry but he would be damned before he drank from that skin again.

Forcing himself to move, Enno got to his hands and knees, then to his feet. The rain had passed, the skies brightened, since he had gone into the cave. Shading his eyes against the slanting rays of the sun, he spotted Tapiola lounging on the grass by the stream. That gave him the impetus he needed to begin the climb down. He had a bone to pick with a certain Sami chieftain.

'Blue Man! What did you see?' Tapiola got his question in first before Enno had a chance to attack.

A growl of anger was the answer.

'Yes, yes, you know it now, don't you! You don't have to take my word for it. You're Black Wolf.'

Enno threw the skin at Tapiola, who caught it to his chest. 'What did you put in that water?'

'Something to bring on dreams, let you see more deeply.'

'Something to make me sick!'

'Regrettable. It does have that side-effect. Take it as all part of the test of character.'

Enno had the sudden suspicion that his temper might be marked down as a failure in that test, and more than anything he did want to impress Tapiola.

He sought for a more dignified response, stiffening his back, lifting his chin. 'So there's no permanent harm?'

'Of course not! It'll wear off in a few minutes.' Tapiola waved the matter aside as of no importance. 'But what happened?'

Enno dropped on his knees beside Tapiola, rubbing both his hands over the short curly hair on the crown of his head. 'I don't know what you've done to me but I dreamed as you said I would. I was a wolf running from hunters.'

Tapiola nodded eagerly. 'Yes—I saw that too.'

'I couldn't get the deer I wanted as I had to keep fleeing.'

'Did it not occur to you to turn and fight?'

'Yes, but I couldn't. I didn't.'

'What happened next?'

'I died.'

Tapiola looked startled. 'You died?'

'Arrow in the back.'

'Maybe you should have stood your ground. Running is not always the answer.'

'And died with an arrow in my chest?'

'You don't know that would have been the

outcome. When I dream of you, I see you and White Wolf fighting for us. You don't run then.'

Enno gazed at the horizon, thinking of the miles that separated him from Africa. He'd been preparing to leave but was it finally time to stand his ground? Was he in danger of losing his life if he carried on fleeing?

But the dream gave no promises. There was no guarantee he would survive if he did turn and fight.

15

Toki wasn't sure at first what to make of his hosts. The man—he introduced himself as Pekka—seemed friendly enough, but the twins, Lempo and Aino, were far from happy to welcome him into their family tent. Following her father's express orders, Aino deigned to roast the duck for their guest's supper, but she made sure he realized that every turn of the spit was done with sizzling resentment.

Pekka and Lempo left him alone with his furious cook while they scouted for sign of his pursuers. Toki watched the girl out of the corner of his eye as he tended to the cuts and scratches on his feet and hands. She was older than he had first thought, perhaps only a year or so younger than him. There was something catlike about her, he decided, maybe because of the neat perfection of her small flat nose

and dark eyes, or because she was spitting and hissing with anger. She had not yet forgiven him for lay-
ing hands on her—and for that he decided he liked
her.

'Where is your mother?' he asked, breaking
the silence. He could see no sign of any other
women in the camp.

Aino hesitated over whether or not she would
allow herself to be lured into conversation, but, for
all her display of resentment, she was curious about
the stranger. So rarely did anyone or anything interesting enter her life. 'Our mother died a long time
ago.'

'I'm sorry.' Toki knew what it was like to lose a
mother; no one had ever adequately replaced his
and she had died sixteen years ago.

Aino shrugged, as if to say a stranger's sympathy was entirely unwelcome.

'You here alone with your father and
brother—just the three of you?'

She nodded. 'We are looking after the camp
until the others return in autumn. They call in from
time to time; they're not far.'

'How many others?'

She flicked a suspicious glance at him. Her
eyes were remarkable—dark and fathomless like the
sea on a winter night, so unlike the pale blue eyes

that ran in his family. 'Why do you want to know these things about us?'

'I'm just interested. I've never travelled this far north before. I'd like to understand how you live.'

'We'd live better without Vikings.'

'But you speak my language. You speak it well.'

'You cannot trade without knowledge of the Norse tongue—we speak it because we have to.'

'But I thought Vikings did not come here.' He gestured to the land beyond the tent entrance.

'Not often—and when they do they are not made welcome. We go to them to sell our goods.'

Toki stretched out on his back, relishing the first chance to rest after having been taken captive. He was enjoying the company of the fierce Beorma girl and had a mind to tweak the tail of this cat.

'Are you married?'

'No.' The spit squeaked as Aino gave it a violent turn.

'Promised to someone?'

'Not yet.'

'So what's wrong with you?'

'Nothing! I'm but seventeen years old.'

'Past time you were engaged then. No one in your tribe want to take you off your father's hands? Hardly surprising if you go round dressed as a boy all the time.'

Aino stabbed the duck with a skewer. 'You are rude, Viking. I could be married but I don't wish it. Father needs me.'

Toki made a sceptical noise. He didn't know exactly why he was baiting her, it felt good to be able to converse with someone without fearing for his life.

'What about you, Viking? Married?'

Toki rolled to his side and propped his head up on his arm. 'No.'

Her lips were curved in a hard little smile. 'None of the girls want you? I'm not surprised. You steal from them too?'

'Believe it or not, that duck was the first thing I've ever tried to steal.'

'Now why wouldn't I think you are telling me the truth?' She tapped her cheek, eyes mockingly round and wide. 'Oh, maybe it is because you are one of those cursed Vikings who make their fortunes taking what's not theirs.'

Refusing to be riled, Toki flopped on his back and laughed. 'I think I like you, Aino Pekkasdottir.' He couldn't help thinking that she was exactly the kind of girl he had always imagined being his helpmate: someone to tease and fight with. He had already begun to fantasize what it might be like making up.

169

'But I don't like you.' Moving stiffly, like a cat doused in cold water, she went to the opening to call her father and brother in for their late supper.

'Then I'll just have to like you enough for both of us, won't I?' He leant forward and snagged a piece off the roasted duck and took a savoury bite. 'Hmm, and she can cook too—is there no end to her virtues?'

'Shut up, Viking—or I'll stuff the duck somewhere you won't like.'

'And such a silver tongue. A true lady of the north. My sister would enjoy meeting you.'

Aino let the tent flap fall back in place. 'You have a sister? How did she survive having you as her brother?'

'She has no complaints—she loves me.'

Carving the duck on to four wooden plates, Aino didn't notice that Toki's face had clouded with grief. 'In that case, she must be mad. Where is she? Perhaps I should have words with her to set her straight about you.'

'I . . . I don't know.'

Aino looked up, hearing the distress in his simple statement. 'I'm sorry. What happened?'

'I . . . left her to die. Alone.' Toki's lips curled with self-disgust. 'Gods, I'm sorry. I'm lying here in comfort, enjoying myself, teasing you, and my sister is . . . my sister is probably dead because of my actions.'

Aino had been determined to dislike their visitor but she could not ignore the raw pain in the Viking's voice. 'I can't believe you had any choice in the matter. Only force would keep you from her—I can tell that you loved her dearly.'

'Yes.' He cleared his throat. 'Yes, I did.'

She knelt at his side and hesitantly placed her hand on the back of his. 'And I'm sure she knew it.'

He nodded, blinking back tears. He hadn't cried since his mother died and refused to do so now, especially in front of strangers. He curled his fingers around hers. 'The worst of it is that she might still be alive—I don't know if I should grieve or not. And if she did survive, then I have to find her. My enemy has decided she might be useful to him.'

Aino squeezed his hand. 'And you will find her, Viking. I can see it in your face—nothing will keep you from her.'

He returned the pressure. 'Please, Aino, call me Toki. I'm tired of being "slave", "boy", or "Viking".'

'All right, Toki.'

The tent flap flicked back into place with an angry snap.

'Kalma's corpse, sister, I thought we agreed that he was a thief and not to be trusted and here you are all over him.' Lempo threw his hunting gear into the corner and kicked off his boots.

Aino jumped up, her cheeks flushing as she realized she had shown a softer side to her character than she had intended. 'I wasn't all over him, Lempo, so don't you go spreading lies!'

'You were holding his hand and practically sitting in his lap!'

'I was . . . I was . . . ' Aino floundered for an explanation.

Emotions back under control, Toki sat up. 'I was upset and your sister was kind enough to offer me comfort.'

'Oh, comfort was it?' Lempo snorted.

'Careful.' Toki's tone was ice. 'Show disrespect to your sister and you'll have me to deal with.'

Aino's embarrassment shifted to anger. 'Keep out, Viking. You've been here five minutes and you stick your nose in where it isn't wanted. This is between my mule-brained brother and me. Anyway, he does nothing but disrespect me—it's what we do.'

Lempo, mollified by this evidence that Aino still sided with him, pounced on his sister and wrestled her to the ground in a puppyish brawl, tickling her ribs. 'That's right, Titch, I disrespect you each time.'

'Get off me, you idiot, or Viking boy here might rip your throat out.'

'Nah, he won't. He's too busy eating to worry about you.'

Toki paused, the betraying drumstick halfway to his mouth. 'I couldn't wait. I thought I'd leave you two to provide the pre-dinner entertainment while I dived in.'

Aino shoved her brother off her and jumped to her feet, pulling her tunic straight. 'Have you no manners?'

'Usually, but I haven't eaten for two days—and wasn't given much before that.'

'Why didn't you say?' Aino began piling more meat on to his plate, adding some flat bread to the serving.

'I thought the duck-stealing was a bit of a give-away. By Odin, this is good.'

'I've got some apple sauce—made from the last of our stores.' She ladled a generous helping beside the bone he had already stripped.

Lempo held out his own plate and tapped it. 'What about me?'

'Serve yourself, you lazy oaf. I'm going to get some mead for our guest.' Aino ran out of the tent as if Toki would fade before her eyes if not fed and watered immediately.

Lempo tugged the other drumstick off the bird. 'Stay away from my sister,' he said with narrowed eyes.

'You should not make her apologize for her kindness,' Toki replied easily, not wanting to give the boy an excuse to pick a fight.

'Just stay away.'

The tent flap pushed open, letting Pekka in.

'We've got company,' he announced briskly. 'A party of four men and a tracking dog approaching fast from the sea. Your pursuers, Viking?'

Toki put his plate aside. 'Aye. I should go before they find me—and I think you should hide too—they take captives wherever they find them.'

Pekka grabbed a bag from a hook on the tent pole. 'They are moving quickly, without burdens. I think they have your recapture in mind rather than looting. The livestock—or most of it—will be safer in the paddocks. My guess is they will pass through if they think you've gone on up the valley. Lempo, go and lay a trail that a blind man can see that suggests just that. No harm if it heads them out towards our traps.'

Lempo threw a fur over his shoulders and tugged a hood shaped like a bear's head over his own before disappearing into the grey night. From a distance he did look like a bear as he pushed his way through the undergrowth.

'So that's how it's done,' whistled Toki appreciatively. 'Not magic—woodcraft.'

Pekka chucked a second skin in Toki's direction. 'Put this on. I'll show you where to hide.'

Toki caught it, but held it uncertainly to his chest. 'But I can't: I'm putting you in danger as long as I stay here.'

Pekka gave an impatient gesture. 'Put it on. Life is dangerous. Those men are a threat to us with or without you.' He glanced around the tent. 'Where's Aino?'

'She'll be back in a moment. She said something about getting mead.'

Pekka swore and ran for the door. 'Then she's gone for the brewery by the boathouse. The men are coming up the river—they're heading straight for her.'

Unaware of the danger outside, Aino was decanting mead from the barrel into a wineskin, humming to herself. The sweet smell of the alcohol filled the tiny wooden shack, reminding her of the honey they had used to make the brew. They'd need to find another hive soon if they wanted to start a new batch. She had a shrewd idea that the bees had nested in the old tree upriver; she'd take a little trip out there tomorrow if her father could spare her, see if her hunch was right.

The light through the open doorway suddenly dimmed.

'Now, now, what do we have here?' A huge Viking stood between her and freedom.

Aino dropped the skin, spilling mead over her feet; she groped for the knife she normally kept tucked in her belt. It wasn't there. She'd left it behind when carving the duck. She converted the gesture to a non-threatening smoothing of her tunic.

'What do you want?' she asked coolly, plugging the tap in the barrel. She tried to act as if strangers creeping up on her was an everyday occurrence.

The man ignored her question, seized her arm, and pulled her outside to where his companions waited.

'What are you? A Beorma?' he asked, giving her a shake.

She attempted to tug her arm free but his large fingers circled her wrist like a manacle. Angry with herself for being caught unawares, she wished she could shout a warning to the others.

'Just answer the question.'

'Yes, I'm a Beorma.'

These must be the men after Toki, she realized: great, big Vikings with the weather-beaten features of seafarers. The feet of the man holding her made her own look tiny, his soft leather boots cross-gartered to legs the size of tree-trunks.

'They're not so fierce after all, hey, Sulke?' He pushed Aino towards their leader. Off-balance, she almost tripped over the wolfhound at his heels. The dog snapped at her, tearing a chunk from her tunic.

'Let go!' Sulke gestured the wolfhound to sit. It whined in protest. 'I told you the stories about the Beormas were exaggerated, Kleppe. How many of you are there, girl?' he asked, squeezing her upper arms painfully.

'Hundreds,' she spat.

'That was a mistake,' he said coldly, wiping his chest where her spittle stained the cloth. 'I had a mind to be kind to you; now you will regret your rash temper.'

Kleppe stepped in. 'Don't kill her just yet, Captain. Ask her about the boy.'

Sulke bared his teeth. 'I was just getting to that. Have you seen a Viking in these parts—a youth, tall, sandy-haired, brown tunic?'

Aino's eyes were shooting sparks. 'You ask me to help you when you've just said you plan to kill me!'

'Ah. But there are ways of killing—you know that. There's short and painless—and then there's the alternative.'

He was serious—she could see it in his eyes. Aino's throat constricted with terror; she struggled to draw breath. 'I . . . I don't know who you're talking about. You're the only Vikings I've seen in my life.'

'Wrong answer. Try again.'

'W-what do you want me to say?'

Sulke brushed his fingers along her jaw, frighteningly gentle. 'I want this mouth of yours to say where you saw him and which way he headed.'

Her voice came out as a whisper. 'Saw who?'

'Oh dear, dear. Like that, is it?' He jerked his head to the wolfhound. 'You want me or him to make you talk? The choice is yours.'

'Please! Don't hurt me.'

'It's far too late for that, little Beorma. Far too late.'

Pekka and Toki crouched in the shadows of the boathouse watching Aino being bullied by the four Vikings. They hadn't hurt her yet, but they were gearing up for it; Toki had seen it too many times to be wrong. The problem was two men could not take on Sulke's party and still hope to get Aino out alive.

'If we rush them, what will she do?' Toki asked Pekka.

The Beorma was furious, his anger an almost tangible heat as he fought his urge to charge straight to her rescue. 'She'll try to get to a weapon. She is probably searching for possibilities even now. I've trained her well. But as you know, she's not strong.'

'If you order her to run for it, would she?' Toki had come to think that sacrificing two lives to save hers might be the only answer. At least it would even the score: a life saved for Freydis lost. He would give himself up but that would not stop the pirates killing the Beormas.

'I doubt very much she would leave me. She'd only run if I was on her heels.'

'All right then: you go in, pull her out, and I'll keep them off as long as possible.'

'It would help if we took out a couple of them before we made the attempt. My spear and a well placed arrow?'

'With that much warning, they might kill her before we can reach her. And the dog might give us away—it's got my scent already. We could use some kind of distraction.'

179

Pekka nodded and thumped Toki on the back. 'I know just the thing. Stay here. Step in if they . . .' He waved his hand towards the Vikings, who were now pushing Aino between them in some vile game.

'They won't harm her on my watch,' Toki promised.

The Beorma slipped off into the undergrowth along the bank, circling back round to the tents. Toki strained to hear what Sulke was saying. He caught fragments of words—threats, curses, insults. Aino managed to look both terrified and furious— he knew that feeling well having spent the last weeks as Sulke's captive. He itched to charge in and stop them but, armed only with a knife and axe, he was vastly outclassed by the sword-carrying raiders. But he would do so if the tormenting turned any nastier.

Aino had taken to insulting them in her own language.

'You are all sons of pigs! Filth!' she hissed at them from the ground where they had pushed her.

'I think the girl is not being very polite to us,' grinned Sulke. 'I like that—a bit of spirit. Perhaps we should make her a slave rather than kill her. What do you think, Kleppe?'

'I'd prefer you to kill me, you dog!' she cursed

in Norse.

Sulke laughed. 'I know you would. That's rather the point. Come now, enough of this. Where's the boy?' He gave her a kick in the ribs—not hard enough to do much damage, but enough to make her fear more punishment. The wolfhound yelped with excitement.

'I haven't seen anyone.'

'That's a shame for you because that would mean you are of no more use to me.' Sulke shook his head in mock sorrow.

Kleppe knelt down and looped his hands around her neck. 'You should have spoken, sweeting.' His thumb touched her pulse—it was racing wildly. But before he could increase the pressure, movement caught his attention.

'What in Loki's name is that?' Kleppe leapt back from Aino and drew his sword. Ambling towards them was an enormous black bear, dark eyes fixed on them, paws thumping on the worn grass in a strange kind of gallop. If it hadn't been so undeniably a bear, its approach could almost have been construed as friendly, like a family dog greeting a master's return. The wolfhound growled, fur on end, as it backed away from a much more powerful foe.

Aino rolled free, putting the Viking between her and the family's domesticated bear, Hero. Raised by the twins from a cub, the creature didn't realize he wasn't human—and right now he was heading straight into a slaughter and there was nothing she could do to warn him.

A spear sang overhead, burying itself between the shoulder blades of the Viking to her right. He sagged to his knees with a grunt of surprise.

'Aino, run!' her father shouted as he leapt over the body to engage a second Viking in combat, his axe against the man's sword. The wolfhound bounded to defend his master, tangling with Pekka's legs as it tried to go for his throat.

But Aino had no intention of obeying her father's command.

Close on Pekka's heels, Toki attacked Sulke, heading straight for the leader with a murderous swing. Kleppe just had time to jump in the way. He knocked Toki back with a blow from the pommel of his sword, then aimed a strike at his chest. Toki ducked and stumbled, narrowly missing a swipe from Sulke's blade. Steel cut the ground, kicking up grit, before Sulke wrenched it free.

Chaos followed as the bear joined the fray, bumping into Kleppe in his eagerness to reach his little mistress, knocking the big man down like a skittle. Aino threw herself on top of Kleppe so Toki only had Sulke to battle. She wrestled a knife from the sheath at his belt, but he dislodged her easily before she could use it. She rolled again, this time ending up under the shaggy body of the bear. Hero was confused, his big head swaying from side to side, sorting through whether this was play or an attack. He snuffed her face, smelling the fear on her skin.

'Up, Hero, up!' Aino urged.

The bear lumbered on to his back legs and growled, a deep sound that made the ground vibrate under Aino. She scrambled out of the way, knowing what would come next. With a blind swipe of his paw, Hero raked Kleppe across the chest before the man could raise his sword to defend himself. Unluckily, Hero caught Toki in the backswing, catapulting him into the river with a splash. Seizing his chance, Sulke went in under the bear's guard and drove the point of his sword into Hero's side. Dark red blood gushed from the wound, maddening the bear. One arm limp, Hero used the other to lash out at his attacker. Sulke leapt out of reach, adjusting his grip, looking for the perfect opening to finish off the creature. Jaws snapped, drool flew in the air as the bear howled his fury.

Lempo ran out of the forest, shedding his fur as he approached, bow strung. An arrow whistled through the sky and buried itself in the thigh of the man still fighting Pekka. The Viking fell, just missing death from Pekka's axe that hit the ground where he had been a moment before.

'Retreat!' Sulke shouted, seeing that he was two men down and they were losing the skirmish. He whistled to the wolfhound to move out of range. No one could control the enraged bear. It would be madness to prolong the battle. Three Vikings and one dog fled, Kleppe bleeding from the bear's talons, the third man limping. They left behind the body of the first casualty of the fight, spear still sticking out of his back. Hero tried to pursue but his front limb would not hold him. He went down on his snout and roared his outrage at letting his prey slip his grasp.

When Toki pulled himself on to the bank after his unplanned dip in the river, he found Lempo and Aino hunched over the bear.

'I'm fine. No need to worry about me!' he called, teeth chattering, the excitement of battle still pumping through his veins.

Pekka picked up Lempo's fur and draped it around Toki's shoulders. 'Just give them a moment— the bear's like a child to us. We owe him our lives.'

Toki was a little ashamed for giving vent to his feeling of neglect. 'Will he be all right?'

'We think so. A bear's hide is tough—lots of fat and muscle before the vital organs. He'll hurt but should heal if it doesn't go bad.'

Toki squeezed water from the hem of his tunic. 'We have to leave. Sulke will come back and he has thirty fighting men on his ship and more dogs to track us. Even with your remarkable bear, I don't fancy our chances.'

'Twenty-nine.' Pekka toed the body of the man he had struck with his spear. 'I don't like him fouling our home but we have no time to bury him. Let's roll him into the river and let the sea deal with him.'

Toki quickly stripped the body of weapons and outer clothes. He'd lost his own shoes after the raid and the man was about the same size.

'And us? Where will we go?' He buckled the sword to his belt as Pekka shoved the body into the river.

'To find the rest of our tribe. We can't defend our position here.'

'But how will we reach them? And what will you do with Hero?'

'Take him with us, of course.'

'We can't hope to outrun Sulke going at the speed of an injured bear.'

'Yes we can—if we go by boat.'

Toki eyed the family's vessel dubiously. It looked very flimsy, built of skins stretched over birch ribs.

'It'll hold us—don't doubt it.' Pekka turned to

his children. 'How are you doing with Hero?'

'Almost there,' called Lempo. 'We have the wound bandaged. He only bit me once—he couldn't help himself. That Viking rat struck him hard.'

Aino was feeding the patient berries from a pouch at her waist, his big snout nuzzling her palm. 'These will help him sleep. Let's get him on board while he can still move.'

The three Beormas coaxed the bear into the boat while Toki stood waist deep in the water to steady it. Wet already, he reckoned it was only fair for him to do that task. Well trained, the creature did not panic as the vessel rocked. The boat sank low in the water as Hero stretched out and yawned. He was taking up the entire length of the vessel.

'We'll need a second boat,' Pekka decided.

With Toki and Lempo's help, he dragged a similar craft from the boathouse and tipped it into the water. All were aware that their respite from Sulke could end at any moment. While the men were busy preparing the craft for the river, Aino went back to the family tent to gather stores and a few essentials.

'I've doused the fire and checked the paddocks,' she said on her return. 'The stock should manage for a day or so, I hope. Troughs are full.'

'If we are away any longer, I'll send someone

back to tend them,' promised Pekka, giving her a comforting hug. He still hadn't quite recovered from the shock of seeing her surrounded by the Vikings.

'I just don't like to leave them. Anyone could take them.'

'I know, sweetheart—but the pirates have left us no choice. If we lose the reindeer or my horse, then so be it; I'd rather them than lose one of you.'

When the four of them had settled into their vessel and lashed Hero's to their gunwale, Pekka pushed off from the bank. He and Lempo propelled the boat along using flat paddles, heading downstream.

'We'll stay close to the far bank,' said Pekka. 'Even if the raiders see us, they shouldn't be able to reach us if they are on foot.'

Until they reached the outlet to the sea, thought Toki. Then there would be the *Marauder* to avoid. If they got caught at that point, he would well and truly be back at square one—and would have brought this family into trouble with him.

Some hours later, after a fitful sleep in the bow of the boat, Toki woke to find Aino taking her turn on the paddle.

'Do you want me to relieve you?' he asked, yawning.

'It's a skilled job, Viking. I don't think we'd better risk it.'

'I thought you agreed to call me Toki.'

She dipped the paddle in the dark silk of the stream. 'Toki then.'

He smiled. 'And you don't think I'm up to the task? I also grew up on water, you know. My home is an island.'

'But are your boats like ours?'

'No, not exactly—but not so different that I can't adapt.'

'Ours are light and swift. You'll have us stranded on a bank in a heartbeat if you don't know what you're doing.'

Toki hadn't the heart for an argument. 'Fair enough. It's no hardship for me to watch you doing all the work.' He paused, enjoying the peace of the night after the ugly violence of the skirmish. Aino made a lovely sight, bending in unison with her father as they steered the vessel along the channel, choosing a path where the water flowed fastest.

'So tell me about Hero,' he said. 'An unusual pet.'

Aino frowned. 'He's not a pet. Bears are our tribe's sacred animal. He protects us and we him.'

'Is that why you have bear pits without stakes—to take them alive?'

'Yes.'

'And what then? What do you do with several hundredweight of angry bear when you trap one?'

'We revere them. Do not mock our ways, Viking.'

'It's Toki—and I was not mocking, just trying to understand.'

'We do not kill them.'

'And yet I see your brother wearing a skin.'

Aino's frown deepened. 'You were asking about the pit—the bears caught this way are for our ceremonies. We do hunt them on occasion—as we do all other animals—for these are not the chosen ones sent by the spirit of the wood.'

'And the chosen ones are the ones that fall in the pit?'

'Yes.'

'And what then?'

'We feed them those berries I used with Hero—to make them sleep. Then we hoist them out and take them to our clan meeting ground. We leave them offerings of food and other tokens. Our chief talks to them.'

'Talks to them? That sounds like a dangerous conversation.'

'In the spirit world, of course. He talks to them to ask for their blessing, find out the health of the forest, how severe the winter will be—the usual questions.'

'And after the conversation?'

'Then they wake up and leave. We track which exit they take from our stone circle—this too is an omen. Last month the bear went through the black fangs so we knew there was going to be trouble.'

'A bear predicted Sulke's attack? That's some creature!'

Aino gave an angry flick to her plaits. 'Ask Papa if you don't believe me.'

'I do believe you—I'm just finding it hard to adjust to the idea of creatures telling us these things about our world when they are so much part of the wild.'

'It's not so strange: all things are connected in the spirit realm.'

Toki pulled the dead Viking's cloak more firmly about his legs. He did not like the smell of it—a mixture of blood and the man's scent lingering after death—but he could not afford to indulge in squeamishness.

'And what about Hero? Do your people have many bears like that?'

Aino's face lit up, her irritation with him forgotten. 'No, we are the only ones. We are counted greatly blessed by the rest of the tribe. Hero's the main reason why we were given the task of staying to tend our winter quarters this summer. And look how he saved us today! The Spirit of the Wood smiled on us when Hero tumbled into a trap.'

'I have to agree—that was a stroke of good fortune.'

'He was tiny when we found him, too young to be able to take care of himself. Papa, Lempo, and I volunteered to raise him—you can hardly believe what a difficult baby he was! We barely got any sleep for weeks. Now he likes to live in a pen by the forest edge—we built him a kind of cave there out of logs. He ambles in to see us several times a day but looks after his own needs now.'

'He's amazing—so gentle with you.'

'We're his family.'

Toki fell silent. He admired Pekka and his children, appreciated the easy way they worked as a team, even to the extent of raising a bear cub together. Their obvious love for each other was so different from his own home where he had always felt like the glue holding his father and Freydis together while they pulled the family apart.

No, that wasn't fair to Freydis: she didn't pull, she had been pushed.

'Do you know where we are going exactly?' Toki asked.

Aino shook her head. 'I only know that the chief took a fishing party to the coast. The cod are in our waters at this time of year.'

'Then we'll have to get past the *Marauder*.'

'Papa will think of a way.'

Toki suppressed any signs of his doubt, not wishing to offend her. No watchman worth his ration would let their little flotilla of two boats go past unchallenged even if they did reach Sulke's vessel before the captain returned.

16

At the entrance to her tent, Freydis strummed her lap harp, picking out a new tune she had running in her head. The people of Tapiola's tribe loved their music, singing long complicated chants far into the night as the clan gathered around the fire. At first the songs had seemed repetitive as they used only a five tone scale, but then she had realized that there was much more to the music than she first thought. The simple building blocks were crafted into pieces that mirrored the land—jumps for mountain peaks, smooth streams of water for rivers, cascades of notes for waterfalls. Freydis was now trying to bring the same qualities to a song she had composed but the results so far had not satisfied her.

'Your music sounds odd.' Tuoni paused by her chair to offer his verdict uninvited.

'Thanks,' said Freydis sourly, trying to fix an

aloof expression on her face while she wished he would get out of her light.

'I didn't mean that I wasn't enjoying it.' He sifted his hands through his hair, pushing it back from his face. 'I think it's wondrous—different— new.'

Unbending a little at the praise, Freydis plucked the notes in a long descending scale, showing off the abilities of her little harp.

'I'd like to be able to do that. Can I have a go?' Tuoni held out his hand, clearly not expecting a refusal.

Freydis passed him the instrument, wondering what he was planning to do next to impress her. Tuoni settled cross-legged on the grass and twiddled his fingers in the air.

'So, you just run them over the strings?'

'Yes.'

Tuoni twanged the harp, grimacing as the notes deadened on his fingertips. 'That doesn't sound right.'

'It takes practice.'

'I'm usually good with instruments.'

'With the pipes and drum, maybe, but this is in a class of its own.'

'You've convinced me. Now show me how to do it.'

She rolled her eyes at his peremptory tone but gave him the lesson he requested. Ten minutes and one passable chord later, he handed back the harp.

'Play me something.'

Freydis settled the instrument on her knees. 'Doesn't it cross your mind to say "please"?'

Tuoni looked up, genuinely surprised. 'What do you mean?'

'Play me something, *please*. Teach me, *please*.'

'Oh.'

'Yes, *oh*. I've noticed you talk to all the girls like that, as if your attention is a great favour and they are lucky to receive it.'

He flashed her a grin. 'And don't you feel fortunate to have my undivided attention right now?'

There were times since her injury when Freydis missed the ability to storm out of someone's presence—this was one of them. Instead, she opened her eyes wide and gave him a soulful look. 'Do you want a truthful answer, Tuoni?'

He nodded, leaning a little closer. 'Of course.'

'To be absolutely honest with you—no.' She plucked the harp harshly right in his ear.

He flinched, his shock evident. 'No?'

'You've got it.'

'But you're supposed to . . . ' One look at her

face and he reconsidered what he was going to say. 'You're supposed to like me.'

Freydis laughed. 'You mean, someone's told you that I've fallen for your irresistible charm?'

He scrubbed the back of his neck awkwardly. 'Well, yes.'

'Check your omens, Tuoni. Adoration and hopeless devotion are not in your future as far as this girl is concerned. Anyway, who told you such a stupid thing?'

Tuoni couldn't help himself; his eyes flickered to Blue Man standing with Tapiola at the entrance to the chief's tent, arguing over a waterskin that they held between them.

'I see.' Freydis silently vowed she would get her revenge. How could Blue Man be so heartless as to set her up with other boys when it was him she liked! 'Well, we'll soon put him right, won't we?'

'We will?' gaped Tuoni.

'Give me your arm. If we don't hurry, he'll leave before I can catch him. He's been getting very good at avoiding me recently.'

'And that's a bad thing?' Grudgingly, Tuoni held out his arm and helped Freydis across the beaten patch of earth that lay between the tents.

'Blue Man!' Freydis called loudly, attracting more than her quarry's attention; half the tribe had paused to watch the Viking girl pounce on her slave.

'Not now, Freydis,' said Enno with a pained expression. 'I'm not feeling so good.'

'And you'll feel even worse when I've finished with you! Did you, or did you not, tell Tuoni here that I was secretly in love with him?'

Enno held his head in his hands. 'Not now, please!'

Tapiola grinned broadly, the lines around his eyes almost swallowing them up.

'Answer me!'

'Well . . . ' Enno resorted to a vague kind of shrug. He didn't think Freydis would like it to be known that he had tried to make Tuoni treat her more kindly.

'It's your fault, you see. Tuoni has been making a fool of himself since you said that—flaunting himself about the camp, flicking that mane of his, pretending an interest in music to impress me—'

Tuoni looked stunned. He hadn't been aware of acting any differently from normal. 'I do not flaunt!'

Freydis put her hands on her hips. 'You do— ask any of the girls. Some of them fall for it but most of us think it's just rather obvious. Sweet of you, really.'

If there had been a sack to put over his head to spare his blushes, Tuoni would have dived for it.

'I can't be responsible for his behaviour,' Enno said, making a valiant effort to defend himself.

'Yes, you can. You encouraged him. The last thing Tuoni needs is to think his good looks have conquered yet another female heart.'

Though he did not appreciate being berated in front of the entire clan, Enno was beginning to find this whole interview rather pleasing. Freydis was declaring she had no feelings for Tuoni and was embarrassing him so completely, he doubted that the boy would dare flick his hair again. And if she didn't like Tuoni, maybe . . .

'All right then, I apologize. Tuoni, Freydis does not admire you from afar—or even it appears from close quarters. You no longer need to act like an idiot in her presence.'

Freydis nodded, satisfied. 'Good. And you promise not to stir things up again, Blue Man?'

'I promise.' His eyes sparkled with pride at her not putting up with any of his nonsense.

Tuoni ducked out of holding her arm by transferring the burden to Enno.

'For the record, Freydis,' Tuoni muttered in passing.

'Hmm?' she enquired.

'I did not pretend interest in your harp. I am interested.'

'Oh.' It was Freydis's turn to flush. 'Sorry. I just assumed . . .'

'Yes, I know. Just . . . don't.'

Tapiola shaded his eyes to watch his grandson slope off up the valley, shoulders hunched.

'Well, little Viking, you pack quite a punch with your words,' Tapiola said, guiding her to a stool in his tent.

'I do?' Her eyes were bright with mischief.

'You know you do. And I think you embarrassed my grandson on purpose.'

She looked a little sheepish. 'Perhaps I did. Sorry.'

'No, no, you are good for Tuoni. He has everything too much his own way among the young people of the clan.'

'I didn't want to hurt his feelings . . .'

'I think he'll recover remarkably quickly and be the better for it.' Tapiola handed her a cup. Enno tried to stop him. 'It's just water, Black Wolf.'

'Blue Man, Black Wolf: how many more colours are you going to collect?' Freydis teased. She loved to see him basking in the respect the Finna tribe gave him. Now her father had gone, the distance between Freydis and Black Wolf did not seem so great as it had between jarl's daughter and slave.

'It's his name in the spirit world, Freydis Ohtheresdottir,' Tapiola corrected her.

'Oh. Well, I suppose it suits him then.' She took a sip.

'Do you want to find out what your spirit name is, child?'

'I don't know. Should I? I mean, what does a spirit name do?'

'A spirit name reveals your innermost nature.'

'So Black Wolf . . . ?'

'Means that our friend here is dangerous. Separated from his pack, he roams the wild. Woe betide his enemy if Black Wolf finds him. He could join our pack—or yours, of course—but his choice is to stay apart.'

'I did not choose my fate!' protested Enno.

'No, but you chose how to handle it. What happened to the others that were taken with you?'

Enno frowned. 'I'm not sure. Many died; a few settled in Ireland, I think; the rest were scattered.'

'But some did settle—cursing the gods, no doubt, but they chose not to stand against their slavery for years as you have, taking the punishment for your stubbornness. Even as a little boy you did not accept what others bent their heads to.'

Enno unconsciously made his hands into fists. 'Tell me why should I accept an injustice?'

'Exactly. You are proud to the bone. Your choice reflects this.'

'So he's Black Wolf,' Freydis concluded. 'I can see that. What do you think I am?'

'I think I know but you have to find it out for yourself, child. This is our way.'

'But I'm not one of you.'

'Aren't you? Aren't all of us part of the same world when you see into the heart of things?'

'I suppose.' Freydis smiled. 'I rather like the sound of that. So tell me, how can I find out this name?'

'Blue Man will show you.'

Enno started. 'Me? You want me to take her there?'

'Yes.'

'Only so she'll blame me for her headache. You're afraid of her tongue, admit it, Tapiola.'

'Perhaps.' The old man chuckled. 'Here, take this with you.' He held out a second waterskin. Enno suspected he had already tasted of its contents. 'And help her make the climb. It is usually done alone, but this time . . . this time, your assistance would be fitting.'

201

* * *

Enno didn't wait at the bottom of the hill as Tapiola had done, but stood on guard at the entrance to the crawl hole. His fingers tapped his thighs restlessly. The mountain had swallowed Freydis completely; he couldn't even see her feet; but he knew she was still in there because she was humming to herself. The drink that had made him dream seemed to have made her drunk. He was going to curse Tapiola if he had to carry her all the way home.

She had been in there for hours. Enno felt the creep of anxiety up his spine. Was she all right? Would it matter if he interrupted her, break the dream-spell? Rubbing his hands over his face, feeling the familiar bumps of his warrior markings on his skin, he told himself not to worry. What could go wrong when she was lying in the cave only feet away from him?

At once, his overactive imagination started suggesting possibilities. It was strong magic they were dealing with here. Perhaps the spirit of the cave thought to hurt the little Viking? Maybe it was a trap Tapiola had lured her into with his promises of one great big happy family across the veil to 'the heart of things'? It was a well-crafted enticement for a girl who was essentially alone.

He couldn't help himself. He leaned down to the entrance and called:

'Freydis! Are you all right?'

Her sweet voice sang, winding in and out of a melody he had never heard before, something about trees climbing to the heavens, clouds scraping the mountain tops.

'Look, if you don't answer me, I'm coming in to get you.'

'*Black Wolf, strong heart,*' she sang, '*wild as a winter storm.*'

'Was that an answer?' Enno wondered at himself, listening to the ramblings of a girl under the influence of that wretched brew of Tapiola's. He should just leave her to sleep it off.

'*Enemies surround the stockade,*
but the wolf saves us.'

'What's that?'

'*Ships sail into the blood-soaked dawn,*
souls sent to the depths.
One rises with a whetted axe
to shatter the warriors on the whale-road.
Changing the course of a kingdom,
the churl's challenger forfeits all.'

The distant quality of her voice made the hairs on the back of his neck prickle.

'Look, Freydis, that's beyond enough. I'm going

to pull you out.' But he couldn't. He'd risk further injuring her leg if he tugged her too hard. 'Please, stop singing and talk to me.'

There was silence in the cave—a big improvement on the haunting song.

'You heard me singing?' It was Freydis's voice—her normal voice.

'Yes, I damn well heard you singing, you daft Viking. You had me worried.'

'You were worried about me? That's nice.'

He heard shuffling noises and after a moment, two tiny shoes appeared in the sunlight, followed by the rest of his mistress. He helped her straighten her tunic over her leggings and then sit upright.

'How's the head?'

'Fine.' Freydis rubbed her eyes, looking more like someone awakened from sleep than a girl with her first hangover.

'There is no justice in this world.' Enno addressed the grey clouds cloaking the sky.

'What?'

'I emerged with the mother-and-father of a headache; you come out looking as if you've had the best night's rest.'

She laughed. 'And what's unfair about that? To be honest with you, I do feel a little confused still.'

'Just confused? You don't feel as if Thor is bashing on your head with his hammer?'

'No.'

Enno sighed and brushed her hair off her face where it had caught on her pale lashes. They were standing close—too close, in truth. He couldn't help but put his arms around her and lean his brow against the top of her head. There was no one here to see, no Viking, no Sami, just the two of them. 'So tell me about this confusion of yours.'

Spots of rain began to fall, stippling the stones of the cave-sanctuary.

She snuggled closer and hoped he wouldn't let go just yet. In his arms, she'd finally come home, like a ship that had made harbour after a long and difficult voyage. 'I heard this song—it came from me and it came from the pictures—we wove it together. I'd already been thinking about it earlier today—before Tuoni came to my tent—but it just wove together in there.'

'Go on.'

'I could have sworn it was only in my head—but you said I was singing aloud?'

'Yes, you were. Something about ships at dawn and a challenger forfeiting his life.'

She nodded slowly. 'That's right. Those are the words that came to me. You were in it. I could see you in your black wolf form. You were fighting a serpent.'

He stifled his uneasiness. 'And I was victorious, I hope? Not that I believe in fortune telling.'

Freydis wrinkled her brow. 'I . . . I don't know. It was . . . it was not clear.'

'Then I beg you to make up an end where the Black Wolf triumphs, snapping off the head of the serpent. That's the conclusion to your story that I would like to hear.' He let his fingers drift through the pale silk of her hair.

'I . . . I can't . . . it's not a song like others I've composed. It is already finished. I can't change a note.' She pulled herself away from him, a little embarrassed by their intimacy. 'And I have to sing it to Tapiola and the clan—I know that much.'

Enno steadied her as they made their way slowly down the slick stones. Both of them were retreating from the moment when their barriers had been down.

'Why can't you change it?' He was feeling a little irritated—and spooked—by her urgency. Coming after his own dream of death, he was beginning to believe that maybe he was doomed.

'Just because.' She twirled her hands helplessly in the air. 'It has to be.'

He swung her into his arms, crutch and all, to

jump the last steep section. The waterskin bumped at his side.

'It's just the drink speaking,' he announced, more to comfort himself than to convince Freydis.

'No, it was the cave. I loved it in there, Blue Man.'

He had the sudden realization that it felt wrong for her to call him by the name given him by Vikings.

'Freydis, would you call me Enno, please?'

'Enno.' She tested the word like a jewel to be treasured. 'That's your real name, isn't it?'

He nodded.

'Thank you.'

'Don't thank me because if I don't put you down immediately, I fear I'm going to have to kiss you.'

'Me?' She laughed. 'And why is that a bad thing?'

'You and I are worlds apart—you know it.'

She shook her head. 'I'm not so sure. There was one thing the cave insisted on.'

'What was that?' Deep down, some part of him anticipated her answer.

'I am White Wolf. So that makes me—'

'My other half.'

17

The pirates' vessel was still moored in the bay when Toki, the three Beormas, and one sleepy bear arrived at the river mouth. Grey gulls and fulmars screamed as someone on board the raiders' ship threw fish scraps overboard, the birds diving and wheeling to snatch the treats from the air.

'What now?' Toki asked Pekka.

'We hide among the reeds and wait,' the Beorma replied calmly, his flat face betraying no anxiety.

'We wait? For how long?'

'It won't be long. Lempo, you know what to do.'

'Aye, Papa.' The boy slithered into the shallows, holding a small box clear of the water.

'Where's he going? It's not safe for any of us to be on our own. For all we know, Sulke might have his men on this side of the river too,' said Toki.

Pekka nudged the boat into a thicket of reeds. 'I can see no sign of them. Do you?'

'No, but that doesn't mean I can't be wrong.'

'I wouldn't send my son into danger, Toki. Please, trust me.'

Toki glanced at Aino: she too looked unworried by this turn of events. 'Of course, I trust you. But what about Hero? What if he wakes and gives away our position?'

Aino calmly unbraided one messy plait and started to work at the tangles with a stag-horn comb. 'He's fine for a little while yet.'

Toki let out a breath, releasing his jumble of panic and fear at the same time. These people lived here—this was their home turf where they should have the advantage. He needed to let them do what they thought was necessary and stop fretting.

'That's better, Viking. You're learning,' said Pekka with a smile. He passed Toki a handful of cold duck. 'Eat, conserve your strength; we'll need you to be at your best as you're the only one of us with a sword.'

Aino puckered her brow. 'Why did you give him the sword, Papa? You know you've always wanted one—and the man died on our land. Surely the spoils go to the one who threw the spear?'

She was right. Toki realized he had not even

thought to offer the sword to his host—he'd made the arrogant assumption of a Viking that he had first call on a prize ahead of a Sami.

'I may have a right to the sword, but I have never trained with one,' Pekka replied evenly. 'And, Toki, I dare say you know how to use it?'

'Yes, I've had the best teachers; I'm generally thought at home to be skilled with the blade. But your daughter has a point—I'm sorry I did not ask.'

Pekka waved the concession away. 'It was not necessary—and we are brothers now we have fought together. Keep it, Toki, and maybe if we find ourselves in more peaceful times, you can show me how to wield it. For now, I will stick to spear, axe, and bow.'

'And bear,' added Toki.

'And bear,' chuckled Pekka.

Waiting in the shadow of the reed bed, Toki found it difficult to be as still as his companions no matter how many times he tried to control his breathing and unclench his tense muscles. They seemed to give themselves over to the moment, like swans skimming along on a perfect current; his emotions churned like a salmon thrashing to go upstream against the rapids. He was aware that he was only a bowshot away from the prisoners on board the *Marauder* and was frustrated that he was in no position to help them. The captives had wanted him to take his chance and escape—but they were his people, his responsibility.

'They've got many from my village on board,' he whispered at length to Aino.

She brushed the back of his hand. 'I'm sorry.'

'My nurse is among them. Magda. She raised me after my mother passed away.'

'When did your mother die?'

'After Freydis was born.'

'Do you remember her?'

'Bits and pieces. She was a quiet woman, devoted to my father but timid. He took the greater hand in my upbringing whenever he was home from his travels.' He wondered why he was telling her this—telling them both, because Pekka too was listening to their softly spoken exchange. But his mother had been gone so long—and now possibly Freydis too—he wanted to share his memories with someone. He realized he felt comfortable with Aino; even her prickly nature was reassuring as he could anticipate how she would react to his teasing. He liked that fact that she had her own opinions and did not hang back in voicing them. Never one to be slow to like someone, he was slipping into deeper and deeper admiration for her.

'Our mother didn't survive our birth either.

We just had Papa.' Aino smiled at her father. 'He scraped by.'

'With plenty of help from the women of our clan.' Pekka tugged his daughter's plait. 'All of them were full of advice on how to rear the pair of you, I can tell you. I ignored most of it.'

'Yes, and they think you've turned out two boys—not a proper daughter,' added Aino.

'You're not so bad. You can cook, can't you? And weave? So what if you can hunt too? You never know when it might come in useful.'

Toki got the impression that this wasn't the first time they had had this conversation.

'I agree—you know I do,' replied Aino. 'Just tell that to the chief's wife.'

'Mumi never had a sense of humour, even as a girl.'

'I would say she thinks I'm a joke. Keeps her sons away from me, doesn't she?'

'You wouldn't want either of those brutes, believe me. Good in a fight but you'd not flourish in their tents. You need a strong, caring man, Aino, someone at least as clever as you. Mumi's sons do not qualify.'

'Then I'm destined never to marry. The only people with the wit to match me are you and Lempo.'

Pekka brushed a fly off his face. 'Then maybe we will have to look beyond the clan for your mate.'

Toki had been thinking something similar himself.

A flicker on the brow of the cliff overlooking the bay caught Toki's attention. The flicker became flame as a beacon flared into the pale glow of the night skies.

He gripped Aino's arm, tugging her round. 'What's that?'

'Our signal. Lempo's managed to light it even after the rain yesterday—that's good.'

'Signal? Are you mad? We have just told the raiders we are somewhere close by!'

'More to the point, young Viking, the rest of our clan knows that there's trouble. We won't be alone for long,' Pekka explained. 'If we are lucky, they'll be here before the pirates come looking for us.'

'And if we are unlucky?'

'We paddle—fast.' From Pekka's grin it was clear he was not expecting that he would have to take such desperate measures.

Toki threw his hands in the air in exasperation. 'All right. I have no choice but to do this your way. But if you had asked me I would have said that our best hope lay in evading the pirates, rather than forcing a confrontation.'

Pekka's expression shifted, his mouth taking a grim line. 'We will not be safe until this shark has been driven from our waters. To do that we need to show him we are no easy pickings for his scavengers.'

'Tapiola and his tribe ran.'

Pekka shrugged. 'We are brothers of the Finnas, but we are not like them. They are peaceful, like the reindeer they herd; we are warriors, like the bears we hunt.' Digging in his bag, he handed Toki a pair of leather vambraces to protect his forearms; they were decorated with a bear on its hind legs.

Touched by his generosity, Toki let his protests subside. He could not give his host any commands, only the benefit of his experience.

'If it comes to a fight, Sulke will prefer to make a swift strike and retreat if that blow does not knock out the opponent.' He laced the armguards tightly, letting Aino tie the knots. 'He has no stomach for a long, costly battle in which he risks losing his authority over his crew.' He held out his hand, fist squeezed tight closed. 'His hold over them lasts only as long as they respect and fear him—and that has already been dented by the mistake he made with Tapiola.' He opened his fingers. 'He is angry now— so more vicious than ever. Keep those who cannot defend themselves far from the fight.' He cast a pointed look at Aino, hoping his message was clear.

'You need not worry about me, Viking,' Aino said stiffly. 'I know how to handle myself in combat.'

'No, Aino,' broke in Pekka, 'you are going nowhere near this one—and that is an order.'

Toki was relieved that the father was now the recipient of Aino's killing looks.

'Besides,' continued Pekka, 'we have driven raiders away before. We usually do not need to fight.'

'So how do you force them away?' asked Toki, intrigued.

'Oh, they leave voluntarily—and very quickly,' murmured Pekka, half to himself as his mind recalled scenes from the past. 'And if I'm not mistaken, this sea mist is just what we need.' He kissed an amulet hanging round his neck. 'Nakki be praised.'

'Nakki?'

'The water-god,' whispered Aino, watching the mist roll towards them like a slow tide, eating up the headland, making the islands out to sea disappear, but leaving the skies above clear. She tugged a pin from her cloak and tossed it into the water. 'May we be as light as a leaf and our enemies as heavy as iron when Nakki rises.'

Pekka nodded his approval. 'And you, Viking,

you should pray to your gods to protect you in case Nakki does not know you are our friend.'

Toki murmured a quick prayer to Njord, the god of the sea, though he privately doubted that his rule extended this far north.

A wet hand grabbed the gunwale as Lempo dragged himself aboard. He tossed a box to Aino.

'Your flint's better than mine,' he gasped. 'Caught first time.'

Aino tucked her prize back in the sack at her feet, then hugged her brother, paying no heed to his bedraggled state. 'Any problems?'

'None. I could hear the pirates making a fuss when they caught sight of the beacon but they seem at a loss what to do about it.'

'That probably means Sulke hasn't got back yet,' suggested Toki.

'Shh!' Pekka raised a warning hand and pointed to the little beach on the opposite side of the river mouth from their position. Three men were pushing a small boat into the water, a dog leaping at their heels. They rowed to the vessel, shouting a warning of their approach.

'That must be him now. I think this is where the fun begins,' said Toki in a low voice.

'Time for us to get ashore,' said Pekka. 'We'll

leave the boats here. Aino, you are to stay in the cover of these reeds with Hero.'

She opened her mouth to protest.

'This is not about keeping you away from danger; if he wakes and creates too much noise too early, our plan will be ruined, our position given away. I'm relying on you to control him.'

Aino's whole body-language shifted, becoming now a warrior taking her commands. 'Yes, Papa. I won't fail you.'

He kissed her cheek. 'I know, sweetheart.'

'Stay safe—all of you.'

'If this works, we won't need to trade a single blow with the enemy.' Pekka made a bundle of his weapons to hold out of the water; Toki followed his example. 'Let's go.'

Pekka, Toki, and Lempo slid out of the boat and into the waist-deep water of the bay. When they left the sheltered stretch of the reed bed, Toki could feel the contending current tug at his legs, the cold rush of river water meeting the ebb and flow of the sea. It was not hard to imagine that the touch were fingers of the water-god trying to pull him down.

The gods must have heard their prayers, because the current slackened and they were able to clamber up the steeply sloping beach unhindered. Once clear of the water, they unwrapped the

217

weapons, strapped them to their belts and ran for cover. Pekka and Lempo took the bear skins they'd used to protect their axes and cast them over their shoulders, pulling the hoods up.

'Toki, get yourself under this!' Pekka chucked him a bundle of damp fur.

Hidden under the musty skin, Toki wondered what he looked like. Hero's younger cousin perhaps?

Pekka and Lempo were already jogging towards the thicket of bushes and trees that covered the lower slopes of the mountains, two hump-shaped shadows disappearing into the darkness under the branches. Toki picked up his pace so he would not lose them. He could not work out what the Beormas had planned, but they had a clear objective in mind so he just had to trust them as Pekka had asked. He ducked under a low bough, tugging his cloak free of the brambles that choked the undergrowth. A little further in, even the brambles gave up their hold, so thick was the shade under the dense pine trees in this part of the forest. The ground was covered in a deep fall of needles, absorbing his footsteps like an eider-down mattress. The air smelt of resin and slow-rotting pine cones.

The first Toki knew of the others was from a strange sense—a thrum in the air—that they were not alone in the forest. A man with a white bear skin thrown loosely over his shoulders stepped out from behind a tree trunk, appearing with the suddenness of a ghost at an enchanter's summons. The bear-head hood pushed back, his shock of white hair framed a tanned oval face; dark eyes flickered across the group, missing no detail.

'Chief Atcha.' Pekka knelt briefly.

'Pekka.' The chief raised him to his feet and embraced him. He then began talking rapidly in their language.

Pekka replied, gesturing to Toki, then to the *Marauder*, explaining the events of the past day. He thumped his chest with his fist, then thrust his arm out, a move that spoke of sweeping their land clean of their enemy.

The white-furred man turned to Toki. 'Stranger.'

'Chief of the Beormas.' Toki bowed.

'You are the son of Ohthere, renowned traveller and protector of the Finnas.'

It was a statement more than a question, but Toki still felt the necessity to confirm it.

'Aye, sir.'

'They say he is a straight man—not crooked in his dealings with our brothers. If his son is like the father, you are a worthy ally. I confirm what Pekka has already promised: we offer you sanctuary in our land.'

'Thank you, Chief Atcha.' He knelt on the soft earth. 'And I offer you this sword in your service this night, if you will accept me.'

'These men are your enemies.' The chief gestured to the bay where the *Marauder* waited. 'Will you help us drive out the foe?'

'Gladly, though I've no idea how we will do this—us four against so many. And my people are on that ship. I won't do anything to risk their lives.'

'Not four, stranger. We are forty.' The chief gave a whistle and the shadows under the forest eaves resolved themselves into the forms of men—or were they bears? In the curling mist it was hard to tell the difference as the skins covered their faces. The knot of apprehension in Toki's chest loosened. They outnumbered the pirates and had the advantage of fighting on a land they knew better than anyone.

'Come, rise. I accept your service, Toki Ohtheresson. The scouts say the pirates are preparing to land to investigate the signal. They do not come in full strength as they still do not know we are here. You go with me, Viking?'

'Of course.'

Chief Atcha led the way back to the beach

below the signal cliff, beckoning Toki to follow. The Beorma was armed only with a stout oak staff which he used to keep his footing on the steep sand dune. Sliding down in his wake, Toki took a glance behind and realized the other Beormas were not following, but stayed hidden in the trees. Were they planning an ambush?

There was no time to ask because a small boat approached from the pirates' vessel, four men aboard. Mist swirled low across the water of the bay, winding around Toki's ankles as he waited for the next move. Then the skies suddenly shifted and a yellow-green bow split the night from east to west, coloured flames dancing along its edge. The Northern Lights had chosen this moment to begin a flamboyant display.

'Enemies of the Beormas, leave this land!' Atcha shouted without warning, making Toki's heart thump in his chest.

The men in the boat yelled curses in reply and brandished their weapons; the rowers put on a burst of speed.

'If you set foot on our land, I will make it rise against you, bring the wild creatures out of the forest to tear your lungs from your bodies.' The chief raised his arms above his head, shaking his staff, the white fur cloak like wings behind him. He looked as if he commanded the lights above as well as the ground beneath. Toki stood staunchly at the chief's side. He could feel the power of command in the chief's voice; it crackled like lightning striking from storm clouds.

'Kill the savage; fetch the boy!' shouted Sulke from the deck of the *Marauder*. Toki could see him clinging to the dragon-headed prow, watching his men do his dirty work for him.

The raiders were only feet from the beach. Toki let his fur drop to the sand to free his arms. Time to draw his sword.

'Get back, old man, we come for the prisoner and to avenge our dead!' warned the leader of the little raiding party. He jumped from the craft and made the last few strides in the shallows. Shaven-headed, with a long fair beard, he had always been one of the worst tormentors among the crew; Thorgisl the Hammerfist they'd called him. Toki stepped forward, ready to defend the Beorma, but the chief motioned him back.

'You pollute our earth and it rejects you!' The chief threw back his head and uttered a cry, a cross between a howl and a growl. All at once, the forest replied, voice after voice bellowing defiance.

Thorgisl was not slow to realize that he would soon be outnumbered, but with his captain as his audience he wanted to display no weakness. He raised his sword and rushed up the steep beach, yelling:

'The white one's mine!'

But his blow did not fall on Atcha's head as he had intended. Toki threw himself in the Viking's path, his own sword jarring as it blocked the strike.

'Fight me, would you, Ohthere's pup?' taunted Thorgisl. His three companions had now caught up with him. Two went for the Beorma, another to help Thorgisl. Toki found himself defending against a double-pronged attack. Out of the corner of his eye, he could see the chief wielding his staff with dazzling skill, deterring any close quarter assault. Toki stumbled, but turned his misstep to his advantage, driving up under the guard of the second man—a killing slice to the stomach. Thorgisl also took his chance, his stroke catching Toki on the arm he had instinctively raised to defend his neck. The blade bit through Toki's leather arm-protector and blood poured from the wound. To gain time to master the pain and gauge his fighting strength, Toki retreated up the beach, his attacker following, swiping the air with menace.

'I've orders not to kill you, whelp, but that doesn't mean you have to be unscarred,' jeered Thorgisl.

223

Toki wiped the sweat from his brow to clear his vision, blurred by tiredness and pain. He was not going to waste his energies on a pointless exchange of insults, not when he knew that his tormentor was walking straight into a trap for which he was the bait.

The man swung again, coming in low to take Toki out at the knees. He jumped, avoiding the swipe, slashing his own blade high so that the pirate had to duck and roll. Droplets of Toki's blood stained the sand, a grim mark of the battle arena.

Breathing hard, Toki took a quick glance around him, wondering where the Beormas were. They should have reached him by now but all he could see was the chief, still occupying the other two raiders with a fierce display of his mastery of the staff. Toki couldn't afford to rely on anyone coming to his aid with this particular challenger; arriving late would be of little comfort to his corpse.

Thorgisl went for him again, driving him back with a rapid flurry of blows—high, high, middle, low, middle. Toki watched for the signals in the muscles of the man's shoulders and in his face, anticipating each attack.

A feint to the left, then a blow to the right—Toki's sword was there to block.

A swift lock of blades against hilts, hot breath in each other's face, before Toki thrust, pushing the man back. Moving at great speed, he turned defence into attack, using his greater reach against the man's superior strength.

Then, suddenly, it was over.

The pirate's sword did not come up in time and one blow reached target, buried in the man's ribs. For a second, Thorgisl did not realize what had happened, could not understand why his sword had tumbled from nerveless fingers, then eyes locked in disbelief on Toki; he fell back, staring up at a heaven where the lights still danced.

One enemy down, Toki ran back to aid the Beorma chief, but found that Atcha had single-handedly driven the two pirates to the water's edge. Hearing the crunch of Toki's footsteps behind him, he leaped back, out of reach of their swords.

'This land rejects you . . . Tell your captain to go . . . or be consumed by it!' the chief panted.

But behind them, the *Marauder* was stealing closer to shore, prow thrust through the mist like a dragon of old. Sulke was going to ride the ship up the beach, allowing its crew of fighting men to attack in one overwhelming wave.

Emboldened by this knowledge, the two men held their ground in the shallows.

'Run, old man, before I spit you on my sword!' threatened one. 'You cannot swing your staff at us for ever . . . aargh!' His eyes bulged, great circles of horror. 'What in Thor's name is that?' He grabbed his companion's arm and pulled.

The second man gave an inarticulate cry, clutching at the amulet round his neck for protection. Forgetting the boat in their rush to retreat to the safety of the ship, the pair splashed deeper, swimming awkwardly with weapons in hand, thrashing towards the *Marauder*. Toki could hear screams and oaths on board, a desperate order shouted over the tumult; in reponse the rowers rapidly changed direction, spinning the prow away from land. He turned to look behind. Out of the mist loped an army of bears led by the unmistakable form of Hero, white bandage across his chest like a commander's sash. Hero rose on his hind legs and howled his defiance, a sound echoed by his followers. The Beorma fighting force halted some distance from the beach, keeping to the cover of the fog, a threatening shadow at the edge of sight, the wild come to the rescue of the people of this land.

The two pirates from the beach reached the ship but no one paid them any heed or offered help to climb aboard. They hung on to a rope, skimming along behind the vessel like a trailing anchor as the

Marauder completed its turn and headed for the open sea.

Toki threw back his head and joined in the howl of triumph that erupted from the Beormas.

'You're bleeding.' Aino padded to his side, Hero following her obediently.

Toki looked down at his bloodstained sleeve. He gingerly tugged it away from the wound. He hissed at the pain. 'A scratch. I thought you were told to wait in the reeds.'

She shrugged, digging for a clean linen bandage in her bag. 'The army of the wild works best with a real bear—Papa knows that. And when Hero woke up in time, I thought I'd help out.'

'What do you mean "works best"?' Toki frowned as she tied off the cloth around his bicep.

'This is not the first time we've used it to scare off enemies. If you take a close look at our forty fighters, you'll see we aren't much of an army.'

Toki raised his eyes to where the Beormas were gathered around their chief and Pekka. Danger chased away, they were removing their bear skins, revealing a hotch-potch of men, women, and older children, the youngest not more than ten, the oldest pushing sixty.

'So that's how the legends began,' he murmured.

'Yes, but don't you dare tell.'

He checked her work: the bandage was neat and tight but the wound still burned. 'Thank you. And, of course, I won't say a word. I'll just think about it from time to time when I'm alone and laugh at Sulke's men being spooked by a bit of Beorma magic.'

Pekka, Lempo, and Chief Atcha approached.

'All well?' enquired Pekka, indicating Toki's arm.

'I'll live. But tell me, Pekka,' Toki put his hands on his hips, 'what exactly were you doing while I was fighting for my life against two raiders?'

The Beorma had the gall to laugh. 'Watching. Taking my first lesson in swordsmanship.'

'I could have been killed!'

'Unlikely. You outclassed them by far. Lempo wanted to interrupt but I told him that would only break your concentration and do you harm.'

Toki gulped down some water from a skin Lempo offered him. 'Next time, go with Lempo's instinct. I wasn't sure I was going to win that one— I'm not exactly at the peak of my performance right now.' He stretched, feeling the weight of the last few days on his shoulders. 'Gods—what would I give for a good night's rest and some food!'

The chief clapped his hands and two women came forward with some dried meat and bread.

'The best we can do tonight,' Atcha explained. 'We'll rest here. You can sleep without fear: my scouts are watching the ship's progress from the headland. Even with the mist, we'll have ample warning if they decide to return.'

'How so? Can you see through fog as well as conjure the animals?'

'Unfortunately not, but they make enough noise to wake the dead, and sound carries across water.'

Seafog continued to wind around their legs, to Toki a visible expression of the exhaustion threatening to make his knees buckle.

'Then I'll make my bed right here,' he yawned, spreading his cloak and using it as a mattress.

'You fought well, stranger,' the chief said with a definite note of approval as he watched the young Viking stretch out on the sand.

'But I didn't save my people.'

'No, but you have saved your honour by fighting off the one who enslaved you.'

'And your staff-work was something to be seen to be believed,' murmured Toki sleepily.

Atcha bowed an acknowledgement. 'Yes, we made quite a team, Viking, much to my surprise.'

'So it was a test?'

'Of a sort. We have never fought alongside Vikings before, only ever seen them as enemies. We all learnt something new tonight.'

18

Enno was bewildered—even more confused than he had been since the first few days as a Viking captive. He'd fallen for a Viking against all his vows to keep aloof and now they were linked by some strange prophecy made by a seer at the world's end.

After delivering Freydis back to the camp, Enno sought a place to be on his own with his reflections. He retreated to his favourite rock overlooking the sea, knowing he would not be disturbed as Freydis had gathered all the Sami to listen to her song. Normally reluctant and shy, the little Viking had been adamant that the performance could not wait. She was a messenger and she must fulfil her duty immediately. Enno could hear her now, the notes of the harp spearing urgently through the air, reaching even him in his isolation.

Enno paced restlessly. Below him the sea rippled like sapphire silk nailed to the earth by studs of lead-coloured islands. Was what he and Freydis had experienced in the cave the work of demons? Sacrilege? His old teachers would have told him that, wouldn't they?

He wasn't sure of anything now. They had died so many years ago, he doubted that he recalled what they taught correctly. Would they have condemned these people as devil-worshippers or would they have found truth in what the Sami believed? God surely spoke to these northerners as well as his own people—would he use rock and paintings for the purpose?

Enno felt as if his head was going to burst, and he couldn't even blame it on Tapiola's doctored water.

He knelt on the ground, trying to clear his mind for prayer. His teachers had always told him to start with the basics; in any dilemma he was to examine his heart and his mind and ask God for guidance.

So what did he think—what did he feel?

Enno bowed then sat on his heels and turned his face to the sunset, the golden light burnishing his skin with bronze. What he felt was that for the first time he was in the right place, with people whom he could love. Their wisdom had something to teach him, and was not to be ignored. And the vision told him that he had run enough; it was time to take a stand.

A sense of peace stole over him. He was no traitor to his God, not when he followed this course with good intentions. He was not promised safety— shadows of death stretched over both paths if the cave was to be believed—but he finally surrendered to these people, to Freydis.

His old reflex of rejection protested. He'd vowed not to get involved, not to care. If he allowed himself to love Freydis, a Viking, he dishonoured the memory of Am and Kas-Jalfir.

Even as he formulated the thought, Enno knew that he was wrong. His first protectors would never ask him to turn from what he felt for Freydis. She had crept through his defences and taken control of his heart. She did not stand for her father and his kind, the slave-takers and slayers.

Weasel words?

The truth.

The matter settled to his satisfaction, Enno completed his prayer and stood up. Time to seize his destiny with both hands.

* * *

Freydis found it strange to command the attention of the Sami so completely, but ever since she had returned to the camp, made her announcement of name, and sung the song, their manner towards her had changed. Beforehand, they had acted as if she were a priceless glass goblet, something to be wrapped and stored away until the owner returned to claim it. Now she felt more like a hub of a wheel, or the bit on a bridle, an essential piece on which everything else depended. It all came down to the simple fact that they believed her. Her dream, Tapiola said, revealed the future. Her coming to them, just before their hour of need, had been foretold. Now they would need to consult their guardians together, he, White Wolf, and Black Wolf, if he could be persuaded.

'I'm not sure he'll like the idea,' Freydis said, not wanting to dash Tapiola's hopes. 'He wasn't pleased when I told him what I'd learned in the cave.'

Luonno and Paiva, the two women who had waited on her since her arrival, entered the chief's tent and placed an enticingly scented bowl of fish stew in Freydis's hands.

'You keep her talking and singing too long,' Luonno scolded Tapiola. As one of the chief's younger sisters, she numbered among those few who felt no need to curb their tongue around him.

Tapiola shook his head, eyes crinkling with humour. 'You underestimate her, Luonno. Freydis Ohtheresdottir is a formidable soul. A little music-making will not weaken her.'

Paiva knelt behind Freydis and began to brush her hair with long sweeping strokes.

'White Wolf's pelt is rumpled from her day in the cave,' she explained when the chief raised a brow.

Freydis felt a little embarrassed. It was clear that the women—and many among the Sami—could not do enough for their messenger.

Maybe I've gone from glass goblet to favourite pet, she thought wryly. *But it does feel very good to be stroked.*

The tent flap jerked back and Enno strode in, bringing a blast of cold air with him. Freydis's eyes went to him immediately. He was magnificent, a warrior ready to do battle. The central fire leapt hungrily, making the shadows dance. Tapiola rose and gestured to him to sit beside him.

'Come eat, my friend. I was just going to send for you.'

'I know—that's why I've come.' He surprised Freydis by taking a place next to her, the first open

235

acknowledgement that things had changed between them. Brushing his hand lightly across hers, he took the bowl from Luonno with gruff thanks. 'You've heard the song. What do you think it means?'

The smile on Tapiola's face dimmed like a cloud passing over the sun.

'The guardians of the other world only speak like this at times of great danger. Usually they prefer us mortals to muddle through on our own.'

Enno waved this aside. 'I believe my God speaks to me at all times—and this time I think he speaks through these dreams.'

'I can accept—the guardians can accept—that you remain true to your faith, Blue Man,' Tapiola said gravely. 'Particularly when we agree on the meaning of the message.'

Freydis finished her stew quietly, listening to them debating the likely source of the oncoming trouble. Enno's change of heart was a surprise—in the short hour they had been separated since returning to camp, he had come to terms with being part of a plan plotted by beings beyond their comprehension. As for her, the interference of the other world had never been a difficulty. Her gods did not keep an exclusive club, with giants and dark elves all sharing the immortal realms. Tapiola's spirit guardians had struck her as just another

236

layer in this complex pantheon. But Enno's God—he was different. He threatened to rub all the others out—or did he embrace them, like a mother with many children? Freydis was thankful she did not have to resolve this puzzle as Enno had had to do.

'Freydis, you are the singer of the song. What do you think it means?' Enno touched her knee to gain her attention.

'Sorry, I was leagues away.' She gave him an apologetic smile.

'It's a Viking song you were given, not a chant like those Tapiola's people sing. I think the manner marks the message as yours. We need to know what we face—what do you think that is?'

Freydis ran the song through her head again. It had come to her in the verse form used by the skalds, a strange choice for Sami spirit guardians if they were the ones behind it. 'Parts of it are obvious, I think. You are expected to save us from our enemies.'

'Thanks, I think I got that much on my own,' muttered Enno. It was a huge burden she—or the song—had handed him.

'But who is "us" and who are the enemies?' asked Tapiola.

Freydis frowned. 'When I heard it, I felt as if it

meant us here—you, me, the people outside this tent.'

'"*Enemies surround the stockade, but the wolf saves us*",' repeated Tapiola.

'But what about: "*Ships sail into the blood-soaked dawn, souls sent to the depths. One rises with a whetted axe to shatter the warriors on the whale-road. Changing the course of a kingdom, the churl's challenger forfeits all.*" Whose kingdom is changed? Who is the churl. Is it me?' Enno's tone was combative.

Freydis shook her head. 'You know I would never describe you as a churl!'

'So I'm the challenger?'

'I . . . I don't know. It might not be about you. You are already named—Black Wolf—why give you yet another name we had not heard before?'

Tapiola reached for his drum, made from a hide stretched tight across an oval frame, the wooden rim inscribed with pictures of men and beasts.

'It is the way of these things to remain obscure,' he said calmly. 'The spirits only show us the next steps, not the whole path. We know enough to prepare for danger. I have not forgotten that we only evaded that pirate and did not defeat him. If his raids on our brethren further north yield little, it would be wise to expect him to come back through our waters with a mighty thirst for revenge. That is one danger I can foresee. Let us listen for others.'

He began beating his drum softly, flicking the double-headed stick in his fingers so it caressed the skin, tapping out the world's heartbeat. Freydis cradled her harp and let her fingertips pluck out a theme, wandering through the notes, waiting for a direction.

'Do you have another of those?' Enno asked, gesturing to the drum.

Tapiola stopped tapping, breaking the spell. Freydis lifted her hands from the harp. The chief looked hard at his African guest, pondering the request.

'Here.' He held out his own drum. 'Let your music free, Blue Man. It has been caged for too long.'

Enno nodded curtly, afraid that he would give in to the emotion welling up in his breast if he spoke. He took the drum and placed it between his knees, refusing the stick. Patting the surface he listened for the tone, explored the potential of the instrument. Finding his way, he started to beat out the rhythms he remembered from his village, and heard on occasion during the early days of his exile when he was still among his kind.

'Join him, White Wolf,' urged Tapiola softly.

Freydis swallowed against the lump in her throat. Enno's face had transformed as soon as he had touched the drum, revealing a more vulnerable person inside. Quietly, she began to improvise on the tune she had composed earlier, fitting it to the beat he set. It changed, became faster, more heated. The words she had heard in the cave whirled in her head but it wasn't her voice that started singing. The tent was filled with the deep, mellow voice, chanting in a language she had not heard before. She did not need to understand the words to know that it was a song of loss, a lament for a country he might never see again.

When the last notes of the harp faded and the drum fell silent, the three sat without speaking for some time.

'That was beautiful. You told me you sang like a frog,' said Freydis, swallowing another lump in her throat.

'Then the frogs in his country sing like song-birds,' declared Tapiola. 'It was good to hear your true voice, my friend.'

Enno couldn't reply. His urge to sing had taken him by surprise and he was still struggling with all that it had stirred up in parts of himself that he had kept locked away.

'Did the spirit guardians speak to you while we

240

were singing?' Freydis asked Tapiola, instinctively understanding that Enno needed a moment to regain control of his emotions.

'No, but I think they spoke to our friend here.' Tapiola looked to Enno expectantly. 'Is that not right?'

'I . . . I don't know,' Enno admitted. 'I cannot read the signals from the dream-world as clearly as you.'

'What did you feel then? When your mind is not certain, your heart very often knows the truth.'

Enno sighed, putting the drum on the ground between them. 'That I'll never go home. At least not in the way I thought I would.' He gave Freydis a smile. 'It seems this African is stuck with you northerners.'

'A weaker man would have given up any hope of return many years ago,' said Tapiola.

'Maybe.'

'Perhaps,' ventured Freydis, 'if you are the challenger, the sacrifice is that you can't go home. You are being asked to give up your dream. In a way, I think it is your song.'

'Hmm, the wolf's cry. That seems right,' agreed Tapiola. 'You are now the hero of a Viking saga.'

'But I'm not a Viking,' growled Enno, not liking the turn this conversation had taken.

241

'You've spent longer with the Vikings than with your own people. You dress in their clothes and speak their language. They have helped make you what you are, even if only by calling on your opposition to their ways,' said Tapiola calmly.

'Shut up, old man.'

'You only insult me because you know I am right. Here, have some mead. Drown your sorrows—and let us plan how we are going to prepare to face the oncoming storm.'

Freydis rose to her feet. Sitting too long made her hip seize up and movement more painful.

'I think I'll leave. You won't need me for the drowning-your-sorrows part of the evening.'

She reached down for her crutch but Enno was there before her. He handed it to her.

'Thank you, Freydis,' he said solemnly.

She gave him a puzzled smile. 'For what?'

'For the song.'

'But I thought you did not like the message?'

'No, but it allowed me to sing again.' He kissed her forehead. 'It brought pleasure as well as pain. Goodnight, White Wolf.'

19

The seafog had cleared by morning. Toki followed Pekka, Aino, and Lempo to the headland where the beacon had burned the night before. They carried with them new stocks of firewood to replenish it. Toki threw his bundle on the ground by the cold pile of ash and then turned to survey the horizon. A watchman stood outlined against the sky— the chief of the Beormas still wearing his white bear skin.

'Have the pirates really gone, Chief Atcha?' Toki asked him, shading with his hands against the dazzle dance of light on the grey-blue waters.

'Yes, they were gone before the mist lifted, but you perhaps know better than any of us if they will come back.'

Toki shook his head. 'It is too hard to predict; we must remain on guard. I know that the pirates must be somewhere in the south of my land in a few weeks' time to be at the meeting with the other rebel lords, but Sulke wants revenge and it will not sit easily on him to leave me free. I fear for my people. His anger this morning will be murderous. He has not achieved all he set out to do.'

'Yet he does not leave empty-handed: he has his slaves and your father's goods in his hold.'

'But the house of Ohthere has not been crushed: that was what he wanted. He is a threat to my sister if she still lives.'

Almost as if his words were a summons, a ship appeared from behind an island out to sea. It had a rounded prow and creamy white sail—unmistakably a Viking vessel.

Atcha gripped his staff. 'They have come back! Our trick last night has not fooled them.' He whirled round, cloak billowing. 'Sound the alarm!'

Toki squinted. No, it couldn't be . . .

'Wait!' He clutched the chief's arm. 'That isn't Sulke's vessel. I think . . . yes, it's the *Sea Otter*.'

'*Sea Otter?*'

'My father's ship.' Toki collapsed to his knees, the shock and relief driving all strength from his bones. 'Oh gods, he has come for me.'

Aino ran to his side, worried that he was hurt. 'Toki, are you all right?'

He held her arms then pulled her into a hug. 'No . . . yes! It's my father. He's found me.'

Aino could feel the shudders running through his body—the release of the pent-up tension of the last few weeks. She gave him a hug, then pushed away.

'Come on, you foolish Viking, he won't find you if you don't let him know you are here. Chief, may we light the beacon?'

Toki leapt to his feet, shoving his tumbled hair impatiently off his face. 'Gods! The beacon! How could I be so stupid?' He ran to Lempo and frisked him for the flint.

'Get off me!' squawked Lempo, not understanding the cause of Toki's urgency.

Aino tapped Toki on the shoulder and held out her box containing flint and tinder. 'I think you are looking for this?'

Toki grabbed the box, giving her an enthusiastic kiss on the cheek in thanks, then attacked the flint, cursing when it failed to light. Aino rolled her eyes.

'Let me.' With deft touch, she nurtured a flame and set the fire to the beacon. 'Put on some green wood when it gets going—that will make it smoke,' she told Toki who was hovering at her shoulder, desperate to help.

The chief strode over. 'Yes, you may light the beacon, Aino,' he said with a smile. 'That is if you are sure, Viking, that you invite friends to visit us?'

Aino blushed, realizing she hadn't waited for permission, so caught up had she been in Toki's rush for action.

Toki shaded his eyes again for a better look at the vessel. 'Yes, I'm certain.'

Atcha nodded. 'Then, Aino, you can leave the beacon now. The ship has already seen the smoke and is changing course.' He turned to Toki. 'I hope you are right about that vessel. My people are not strong enough to fight so many Vikings—not in daylight.'

'I know that ship better than any other. I helped build her.'

'Then come with me to the beach. Let us greet Ohthere the Traveller and make him welcome. Pekka, Lempo, Aino, you should join us, because it is thanks to you that the Viking father gets his son back.'

Dazed by this unlooked for turn of fortune, Toki couldn't believe this was really happening. Stumbling behind Atcha, he had to dig his nails in his palm to check he wasn't dreaming. By the time he reached the beach, the desire to see his father again had mingled with anxiety. What would Ohthere say when he knew Toki had failed to defend his home—his family—his people? But then, surely Ohthere knew; how else could he be here?

Did he also know what had happened to Freydis? Had he found her body hidden in the pit? Toki shuddered, afraid of the news that his father might bring.

The *Sea Otter* took the last bend in the sea inlet to bring the sailors in sight of the beach. Toki could see their heads bending as they pulled at the oars. And was that Leif standing at the stern, hand on the rudder? But the man on the prow . . .

As soon as Ohthere saw a Viking boy standing on the beach with the Beormas, he dived over the side and swam to shore, staggering the last paces in the shallows, weighed down by his wet clothes. He was hit in the chest by a warm body before he was clear of the water. Youthful arms ringed him in a crushing hug.

'Father! It really is you! Thank the gods, thank the gods!'

Ohthere embraced his son, rocking him to and fro, uncaring who saw him shed tears of joy. His hands searched his boy's beloved face, shoulders, chest, seeking signs of injury.

'Toki, Toki—praise be to One-eyed Odin! Are you all right?'

'I'm well, Father. Really, I am.'

'I can't believe it—how did you get here—where are the raiders?'

'Gone. You must have passed them in the mist last night.' Toki took a pace backwards so he could see his father's expression. 'They still have our people—I'm sorry.'

'It is not your fault, my boy. We will pursue them—save our people and crush that worm Sulke beneath our boots.'

Toki glanced over his shoulder to where the Beormas were patiently waiting on the beach. He realized then that he and his father were still standing in the sea, soon to be run down by the *Sea Otter* if they did not clear the way for the ship to moor.

'I must introduce you to the people who protected me. Come on.' Taking his father's arm, he guided him up the steeply shelving beach. They were both shivering in the icy water.

'Toki's father.' Atcha bowed. 'Welcome to our land.'

Ohthere returned the gesture. 'I am for ever in your debt, chief.'

'Your son is a fine man, an honour to his family. He acquitted himself well in the battle last night.'

'There was a battle?' Ohthere swung round to his son. 'You fought?'

'Aye, but only a skirmish. Sulke retreated without engaging all his forces.'

Ohthere shook his head. 'I can't believe he gave up so easily.'

'There was a reason.' Toki's gaze flickered to Aino, remembering his promise to keep the secret that defended the Beormas behind a veil of mystery. It felt strange, though, not to tell his father the full truth. 'Our friends here know powerful enchantments; their magic scared him away.'

Having heard rumours in the past, Ohthere accepted the explanation and let the matter drop. He was too eager to hear all his son's news to question what Toki told him.

'Aye, I believe your new allies wield strange magic.'

'And these are my friends, Pekka and his children, Lempo and Aino. They are the ones who first offered me shelter.'

Ohthere held out his hand to Pekka. 'If there is any way in which I can return your kindness, you are to name it.'

'There is no need, Jarl Ohthere. Your son has repaid us many times over with his companionship. We have all become very fond of him during the short time of our acquaintance and do not wonder that his father has come to the ends of the earth to find him.'

'You are right. I would have sailed so the ship scraped the scales of the great serpent Jormungand, to the very boundaries of the sea, and I would never have given up.' Ohthere spoke the last words to Toki, a vow of sorts.

Toki felt his heart expand, bursting with love for his father. If he had ever needed proof of Ohthere's deep affection for him, he had it now.

The crunch of the keel on the beach announced the arrival of the *Sea Otter*. Vikings jumped over the side and sprinted forward to swamp Toki in their enthusiastic greetings. He was pummelled from all sides as they hugged, punched his arm, and tousled his hair.

'My daughter? Is she still alive?' asked one.

'My wife and children—were they taken too?' asked another.

Toki held up a hand for silence. 'I'm sorry: I know I failed you all. I couldn't stop the raiders—there were too many of them. But Sulke takes the women and children as slaves.' Toki spoke clearly, hoping his certainty would comfort those seeking their families. 'They are kept aboard, fed, and given water. Though I wouldn't say that Sulke and his men are kind, the crew do not damage their investment with unnecessary cruelty. We've lost no one else since the raid. And they've been so brave—all of them. They helped me escape—made sure I got a chance to flee. Their courage will see them through this.'

'And we will follow the *Marauder*,' promised Ohthere, standing beside his son. 'Sulke is only a few hours ahead. Lads, you should take heart from the news that we have gained on him.'

The men accepted their leader's word and dispersed to receive the gifts of food brought to them by the Beormas. Sitting in circles on the level ground beyond the sand dunes, they ate and drank in celebration; with Toki returned to them, the dream of freeing the rest of their people no longer seemed so impossible.

Alone on the beach with Ohthere, Toki steeled himself to ask for the news he dreaded. 'Father, what of Freydis?'

Ohthere raised a brow, surprised by the question. 'She lives.'

Toki swayed as relief swept through him; he grabbed on to his father's arm to steady himself.

Ohthere frowned. 'I thought you knew. She said you saved her by ordering her to hide. Did she lie?'

'I left her, Father. Left her in a pit with a terrible wound. I wasn't sure she could climb out alone.'

Ohthere waved away Toki's concerns. 'Of course she was able. Probably pretended that she was worse off than she was so you would command her to hide.' His expression hardened further. 'I made it clear to her that her cowardice did not reflect well on the family honour.'

Toki's heart went cold. He took a step away, letting his hand fall from Ohthere's arm. 'She did not feign her injury—her leg was badly wounded. And even if she had been unharmed I still would have ordered her to remain there out of danger's way. It was just as well I did so because now Sulke knows about her; he mentioned that he would have wed her and seized your lands through her inheritance.'

'Then it is fortunate that I've left her with Tapiola's people, out of the path of other scheming men.' Ohthere held out his hand, trying to bring his son back within reach. 'Don't worry about your sister; she is fine where she is. In fact, now she is crippled, it may be better for all concerned that she stay there. She has become an embarrassment to us.'

'Crippled?' Toki shook his head, trying to make sense of what his father was telling him. 'But you said she wasn't seriously injured!'

'It was a bad enough blow, I suppose.' Ohthere

shrugged, anger gathering that once again his daughter was driving a wedge between him and his son. 'I had the wound cauterized but the bone hasn't set right and she has to use a crutch to walk. It's an ugly thing—a hobbling girl.'

'Is she in pain?' Toki gritted his teeth, knowing it pointless to challenge his father about anything concerning his sister.

'Some, I would guess. I will say one thing for her: she bears her injury without complaint. She would have made a good warrior had she been born a boy. But enough about her, Toki: I want to hear everything that has happened to you since the raid on Bjarkoy.'

Toki held up a hand. 'First tell me you didn't leave her alone with the Sami. Did you make sure there was someone to care for her?'

'Of course,' huffed Ohthere. 'I gave her a slave—a blue man from Africa—a wondrous creature with skin like the winter night.'

'But a stranger?'

'Well, yes. I bought him in Sciringesheal. Not good slave material—far too proud—but he looks after your sister well enough.'

Toki turned away to regain control of his anger. He and his father had never seen eye-to-eye over anything to do with Freydis; he could not shake him from the suspicion that she was not his child. Toki had never understood why his father had so little trust in their mother, unless it was because he had listened more to the malicious whisperings of ill-intentioned neighbours, jealous of the jarl's wealth, than the views of his own family. Toki vowed that he would make sure they returned to Freydis as swiftly as possible and the best way of achieving that was by keeping his desire quiet. To speak out would make his father more stubborn.

Toki let out a slow breath, calming his voice to a reasonable tone. 'Come, Father, let us accept the chief's hospitality and I will tell you all I know about Sulke's plans.'

Ohthere pulled his son back into his embrace. 'Aye, let's do that. By Odin's tree, it is good to see you again!'

Father and son were given a reed mat to sit on and lavished with the best of the food on offer—tender meat, dried berries, and oat biscuits made from precious stores brought in by trade. The Beormas gave them space to exchange news, though Toki kept his eye on Aino, making sure none of the Vikings bothered her. He was relieved to see that the two peoples, Beorma and Norse, treated each other with distant respect; none of the crew was foolish enough to try to be over-friendly with the women, not when the men were reputed to be able to shape-shift into bears.

Reassured enough to tell his news, Toki began the account of all that had happened. When Ohthere heard Sulke intended to meet with the other rebellious lords, he reciprocated by telling Toki about his orders to return with his fighting men to defend the kingdom.

'So Sulke's raid on the north was one strand in a much larger plan?' Toki guessed.

Ohthere nodded. 'I wouldn't be surprised to hear that ours was not the only homestead raided by the pirates in advance of their attack on Harald. They seek to weaken the men loyal to the king. And all of them are fighting among themselves to strengthen their own positions, struggling to see who will come out on top. It galls me to think that my enemy is making his claim with my wealth—my people.'

'But we can still stop him.'

'Aye, we can do that. But we will achieve nothing by sitting here. The action is now down south. We must make all speed either to catch Sulke or, failing that, join Harald to be ready to give battle. So let us thank our new friends and set sail.'

'Father.' Toki put his hand on Ohthere's arm to stop him rising. 'I have a request to make.'

Ohthere sat back and smiled. 'For you, my son, I would fetch the moon from the skies if you asked.'

Toki laughed. 'No, no, it is nothing so difficult to grant. These people, well, they are very special to me. I know you are the protector of the Finnas; now we've come all this way, I would like to forge an alliance with these Beormas too.'

Ohthere creased his brow, considering the problem from all angles. 'But they live far beyond our reach, Toki. We cannot offer them sufficient guarantees of our aid in order to justify extracting a tribute from them.'

Toki shook his head. 'That is not the relation-ship I had in mind. These people have their own ways of defending themselves; they don't need us Vikings for that. No, I mean an alliance, a friendship, bound by . . . well, by a marriage.'

Ohthere threw back his head and laughed. 'I should have guessed! You were always so quick to make up your mind on such matters. Some Beorma maiden has caught your eye! Which one?' His gaze wandered among the women serving the food. 'That buxom one with the red tunic? She's a pretty armful.'

Toki felt his cheeks blush. 'No, I was thinking

256

of Pekka's daughter, Aino. She's over there with her twin brother, Lempo.'

'What! That little boyling? When you first introduced us, I thought you made a mistake. What possessed her father to let her dress like a son?'

'The twins lost their mother when they were little. Pekka treats her as an equal to Lempo.'

'Extraordinary.' Ohthere shook his head in disgust. 'Still, she is attractive enough, I suppose, if you ignore the wrapping. This Pekka, he is an important man in this tribe?'

'He is. He is entrusted with the tribe's sacred bear.'

Ohthere's eyebrows shot up. 'They have a bear? I would love to see that!'

'Yes, he's called Hero and he's quite tame—at least to his family.'

'And your Aino, she also helps tend this bear?'

Toki nodded. 'In fact, I think she is his chief carer. She brought him into battle last night.'

'A bear maiden—yes, yes, this has potential. When the skalds sing her story, the honour of our house will be much increased.' Ohthere thumped his son on the back. 'I understand now. You have chosen well. I will ask the father if he is willing to let you wed his daughter. She has a dowry, I suppose?'

'I . . . I hadn't thought to ask.' Toki had a

sudden sinking feeling that Aino would reject him, that he'd taken Pekka's hints that he was looking for a spouse beyond the tribe too personally.

Ohthere rubbed his hands together. 'Never mind. Leave those details to the fathers. I will talk to him and the chief immediately. If we want to settle the business on this voyage, we have to move quickly: I want to sail before the day grows much older.'

Ohthere got to his feet and strode off in search of Pekka. Toki flopped on his back with a groan. What had he done?

WAR

'I fought alone with eight,
And twice with eleven.
I fed the wolf with corpses,
Killed them all myself.
Fiercely we swapped
blades that shiver through shields.
From the tree of my arm
I tossed the plated fire of death.'

(EGIL'S SAGA)

20

Enno contemplated the Sami camp, planning the best way to defend it against attack. He could not have asked for a safer haven; no foe could hope to scale these cliffs against a determined assault above. Tapiola's people had chosen well.

Turning to the view of Soroy and the other islands scattered on the ocean below, he was less happy. The herds on their summer grazing, and the men guarding them, were much more exposed. They faced an unpleasant dilemma. The Sami could not afford to waste the few short months of sun; the reindeer had to be allowed to roam the islands if they were to preserve the mountain pasture for the winter. If he suggested everyone retreat again for an indefinite period while they waited for news of the pirates, he would be imperilling the herd's survival later in the year, and by extension that of the tribe who depended on the reindeer for their basic needs of food and clothing. Life here was lived on the edge of survival; tip the seasonal balance too far one way and it would not be sustainable. Added to that, the livestock could not be driven to and fro across the sound on a whim: whatever plan he came up with had to allow enough time to secure the tribe's four-footed wealth.

'Is there a problem, Enno?' Freydis hopped to his side, swinging the crutch with ease now. A light-blue woollen cloak was fastened at her shoulder with the wolf-headed pin. He thought she looked wonderful.

'I can't see how we can make them completely safe,' he admitted, putting an arm around her and pulling her to his side. 'As you know, these pirates sneak in fast and from an unexpected direction. Their strike is deadly.'

'Yes, it is, but they won't want a long battle. That's not the Viking way. We should be safe up here.'

'I know that, Freydis.' He gestured to the steep path at their feet. 'Take a look down there—suicide to climb up if someone is holding the fortress against you. This place will not fall without some treachery on the part of the Sami—and I don't think that's very likely. It's the herdsmen I'm worried about. If Sulke raids the island on his way back, it will go badly for them. They are scattered, armed only with hunting gear.'

Freydis followed his gaze to the island of Soroy out to sea, a green jewel on a grey pewter platter. 'But my father will stop him. He went after him, didn't he?' She touched the head of her pin like a talisman.

'There are many sea miles between them. They could pass each other and not know. We can't count on Ohthere to protect us.'

Freydis let go of the pin. 'Well then, we'll have to do it ourselves, won't we?'

'I'm afraid so—and I think I know how we should begin.'

Enno spent the next few days teaching the Sami men all that he had learned about Viking fighting during his years as a slave. Men came in shifts from the pasture, eager to hear what he had to tell them. He demonstrated swordsmanship with a wooden blade as there were no real ones in the camp. He showed them the shield-wall and how two sides could spend many hours locked in battle, shoving to gain advantage and ground over the enemy.

'We do not want to get into this kind of tussle with the pirates,' he warned the twenty or so men gathered for their lesson. 'They are strong, trained for this kind of combat. If they form a shield-wall against us, the best defence is to retreat. Your advantage is that you are on home ground and know how to evade. Fight and run; fight and run.'

Tuoni was his most enthusiastic student, copying Enno's moves with the fervour of a devoted disciple. Freydis noted to her private amusement that he had started decorating his cheeks with black swirls of paint, an echo of the African's markings. Other young men followed his example, until all of them sported the decoration like a badge of honour. She'd even heard them referring to themselves as Black Wolf's men.

Freydis was feeling guilty about Tuoni. He had not spoken to her since the day she had managed to embarrass him. Seeing him practising hard with an axe and shield against a straw dummy one morning, Freydis decided it was time to end the silence. She approached, making plenty of noise with her crutch to give him warning. It was never a good idea to sneak up on an armed man, and certainly not one who bore her a grudge.

'Tuoni!' she called.

He completed his chop, beheading the manikin. 'White Wolf.'

'That looks like hot work. I've brought you some water.' She held out her peace offering.

'Thank you,' he said stiffly.

This was going to be harder than she thought.

'Black Wolf says you are making great progress—he's really pleased.'

She was rewarded with a fleeting smile. 'He is?'

'Yes, talks about you all the time.' That was stretching the truth a little, but he had mentioned Tuoni's dedication.

'He's wondrous—a really good teacher.'

'And it looks to me as if you're a good student.'

Her remark made him frown. 'What's going on here?' he asked, waggling his finger, pointing to her then to himself. 'Why are you suddenly being so nice to me?'

Her gaze slid away. 'I was just trying to make conversation.'

He dropped the shield on the ground, following it with the axe. 'No, you weren't. You want something.'

'I don't! Well, not really. I . . . I just wanted to make things all right between us.'

He turned his back and picked up his outer tunic which he'd left draped on a stone. 'There's nothing wrong that needs putting right.'

'There is—you know it. I embarrassed you the other day. I'm sorry. I'm not expecting you to suddenly start liking me or anything—'

'Not much chance of that, is there? Not with you being a Viking.'

'Well! Of all the stupid things to say!' spluttered Freydis. 'I'm on your side, if you haven't forgotten! Black Wolf and I are helping you defend yourselves against another attack!'

Tuoni flicked his long hair contemptuously as he swept the axe up from the earth.

'As I see it, you and your family are the reason we are in trouble in the first place.' He started walking away, going too fast so that she couldn't keep up even if she had wanted.

'Pig-headed, hayrick-haired idiot,' muttered Freydis furiously.

She heard a familiar chuckle behind her. 'Peacemaking not going smoothly?' Enno stepped out from a row of manikins he had just finished preparing for the next training session.

Freydis blushed. 'You heard then?'

'I heard you try and make peace while the "pig-headed, hayrick-haired idiot" made a fool of himself.' He nodded to the overly self-conscious Sami boy strutting about the camp. 'Look, he's going among his little court of followers, just to reassure himself

266

that all is as it should be in his world. You threaten him, Freydis.'

She laughed. 'Me? How could he possibly persuade himself that I am a threat?'

'Your people are more powerful than his; you have an important role in his tribe; you've already shown you can resist his charm, unlike the other girls of your age.'

Freydis's blush deepened. 'Only because I prefer you.'

'You shouldn't, you know. He's much more eligible.' He moved closer.

'I know, but I can't help myself. I think I was hooked from the moment you told me you wouldn't be my slave.'

He laughed, then dropped a light kiss on her mouth, tempted to take more but knowing they were probably being watched. 'I'll remember you like rebels.'

'How is this ever going to work, Enno?'

'I don't know, love, but we are bound together now. There's no going back.'

'Isn't there?'

'I thought you Vikings knew that.'

'We do?'

'It's there in your carvings and in your jewellery. Even in your music.'

'What is?'

'That the world is interlaced—men bound to animals, linked to gods and to monsters. You to me. All twisting and turning but never reaching an end.' Enno didn't want to mention that the one way the pattern broke was on death; he prayed for her sake that he would survive the coming battle. 'You're the weft to my warp.'

Freydis gave a gurgle of laughter. 'Very elegant.'

'Sorry; I'm not as skilled at words as you.'

She pulled his face down to hers and kissed him. 'No, you are very skilled. Our fates are woven together. We'll find a way to make it work.'

Tuoni, his cousin Jumala, and the other boys who styled themselves Black Wolf's men had grown increasingly restless being cooped up in the hidden camp, forbidden from joining the guard on the reindeer on the island. A few days after Tuoni's confrontation with Freydis, they slipped away, taking Tuoni's little boat to cross to Soroy where Enno had gone to continue his training of the herdsmen. The boys were only halfway, right in the middle of the fjord, when the pirates' ship, the *Marauder*, came into sight, steering directly for them.

'Split up!' shouted Tuoni, realizing that they were sitting ducks in the exposed little boat. He dived over the side and heard two splashes behind him as his friends followed his example. Striking for the island, he swam fast, every moment expecting to feel an arrow between his shoulder blades. He reached the rocky inlet unharmed and scrambled up the shifting pebbles of the beach. Glancing back, he saw with horror that Jumala and another boy had been dragged from the water and thrown on the deck of the pirates' vessel. As he ran for the pastures, he cursed himself for leading the others into danger.

'Black Wolf, they're here!'

Enno turned on the shout to see a bedraggled Tuoni racing towards him.

'The pirates are back. They've got Jumala and Tapio!'

'What are you doing on the island?' bellowed Enno. 'You were told to stay and help guard the camp!'

'I'm sorry—I'm sorry.' Tuoni fell to his knees, panting as if his sides would burst. 'We were stupid—we wanted to help you.'

Enno clamped down on his anger; there was no time for recriminations. The watch that Tapiola had set on the mountain should alert the camp to the danger; his most immediate problem was the herd, wandering unprotected on Soroy.

'We have to pen the raiders in. We must stop them scattering and attacking from too many directions for us to handle. Where are they coming ashore?'

Tuoni pointed back towards the beach facing inland. 'That way. They're coming from the fjord—not the sea. That's where they caught us.'

Enno nodded. He had prepared plans to defend the pasture from every approach. The direction Tuoni pointed led up through a defile between two low cliffs, a place he had already decided was good for an ambush.

'Get your bows and spears. Use your slings too—there will be plenty of rocks to hand on the cliff tops. Kutar,' he pointed to a fisherman who had demonstrated a cool head during practice, 'you take half the men to the south side, I'll take the rest to the north. We'll try and trap them in the gully. If they break out, remember that we mustn't let them pin us down. We have nothing to match their swords.'

'What about my cousin and Tapio?' asked Tuoni desperately.

'They must take their chances like the rest of us. If we can, we will free them, but our first duty is to defend this island.'

Enno wished he had had longer to train the men, but the crisis was already upon them. As they ran towards the cliffs to take up their positions, Enno found himself thinking of Freydis's song. He only hoped the Wolf Cry was right and he would manage to save them.

Once near to the edge, the Sami guard and Enno approached with caution—surprise their main advantage. Going on experience, the pirates would expect them to flee, leaving the reindeer open to slaughter. Stretched out on his stomach, he looked down on the inlet from the low cliff top. It was empty. Where was the *Marauder*? Shifting so that he had a better view of the fjord, he saw it prowling the water separating Soroy from the mainland.

What was keeping them? Raiders usually hit hard and fast; Sulke was wasting precious moments in plain sight.

Then slowly the ship changed course, heading towards the island as Enno had anticipated, approaching with a stately prowl like that of a lion from the deserts of his own country. Using hand signals, he told the Sami to get ready.

The keel of the *Marauder* crunched on the pebbles and men jumped over the sides, swords already unsheathed. They were moving silently and efficiently with the ease of a well-trained crew. At the front was the biggest man Enno had ever seen—black-bearded and a face reddened like a smith at a forge. He wore leather armour and a steel helmet, two slits in the eye-piece and a beaklike nose guard giving him the predatory look of a bird of prey. Enno waited for the man to reach the head of the gully then signalled the attack. With a hiss like wind through reeds, the arrows flew from the hunting bows. Next came a hail of rocks as slings released their burdens. The pirates broke their silence—yells of fury, cries of pain, echoing in the trap.

'Charge!' shouted Kleppe as soon as he spotted the ambush. He intended to break out of the gully and level the advantage with the weaker foe.

Enno took aim and fired. His arrow buried itself in the big man's unprotected calf. The warrior bent down to rip the missile free.

'Slaughter the lot of them!' cried Kleppe, holding his shield over his head.

Order restored, the pirates muscled their way out of the gully, using their shields as a roof against further attack. Two raiders lay dead, caught by lucky shots in eye and throat.

'Remember—keep your distance if they form a shield wall against us!' ordered Enno. 'Archers: cover us!'

At a run, Enno led the spearmen and those carrying fishing harpoons to within fifty paces of the pirates. The Sami knelt down, using what cover the boulder strewn meadow offered. Battle senses sharpened, Enno had a brief, unnaturally clear impression of springy reindeer moss entwined with red twigs, grey lichen-covered rocks and the wet earth. Sami land: their home, which these raiders were violating with their blood-soaked boots.

'The guardian spirits be with them; and my God with me,' he muttered.

He then noticed Tuoni crouching at his side, fishing spear in shaking hand. The boy still looked pale with shock, but his mouth was firm with determination. Enno wished he wasn't here—an added worry to have the boy in the middle of what was going to be a vicious battle—but there was no safety in hanging behind.

'Keep with me,' he said. 'Watch my back.'

Tuoni nodded once, his eyes never leaving the pirates as they ran towards the Sami, axe and sword raised.

Judging the distance close enough, Enno rose and hurled his spear. It struck a stocky fighter in the chest, knocking him backwards. The men behind stumbled over the corpse. Harpoons and spears sang in the wind, shafts thrumming as skills perfected in hunting were turned to men-killing. Still the attackers came.

'Axes!' yelled Enno. He released his own from his belt and shifted a stout round shield from his back where it had been slung. His tools were a joke compared to the well-wrought weapons of the raiders, but they were all he had.

The clash of blades on the Sami shields echoed like a rockfall across the meadow. Kleppe, limping a little behind the vanguard, engaged Enno, hammering at him with his short sword and axe. In contempt for the rag-tag army, the pirate had thrown away his own shield, choosing to attack two-handed.

'What foul creature are you?' he bellowed, swinging at Enno's neck. 'Abomination!'

Enno ducked the over-enthusiastic blow, buying himself a few seconds.

'I'm Black Wolf,' he snarled, as they circled each other. 'Keep away from my pack.'

'Know me then, Black Wolf: I'm Kleppe Wolf-Hunter. I'll wear your skin for a cloak this winter.' The big man feinted with his axe, burying it in Enno's shield, rendering it useless; then he thrust swiftly with his sword, a blow aimed at Enno's heart. To their joint surprise, the stroke fell short, shearing off a shield pushed in its path by

274

a long-haired Sami youth. With a yell of fury, Kleppe caught the boy across the side of the head, slicing ear and cheek with his back swing. Enno pushed Tuoni aside and cut Kleppe's legs from under him with his axe. Not pausing, he palmed a dagger from his belt and buried it in the man's windpipe.

Staggering to his feet, Enno realized the pirates were retreating, dragging the walking injured with them. Those more seriously wounded were abandoned, left groaning and bleeding on the ground. Freydis had been right: the raiders had no stomach for prolonged battles, not when their commander had fallen. The Sami, led by Kutar, were harrying their flight, hoping to free the boys captured earlier. Enno wanted to call them back, fearing the trap was about to be reversed. Only twelve men had been sent on this raiding party, leaving at least this number on board the ship. He raced after the fighters, but found the Sami alone on an empty strand, gathered in impotent anger around the bodies of Jumala and Tapio; the *Marauder* was already heading out to the middle of the channel with men clambering aboard.

'Killed—with a blow to the back of their skulls,' said Kutar hollowly. 'Tapio was my sister's son.'

'I'm sorry,' said Enno.

Kutar swallowed, struggling for calm. 'They stuck their heads in the mouth of the dragon. We should not be surprised it bit. It is not your fault. You saved the herd; you saved us.'

Enno knew that this was true. It should be enough, but it wasn't.

'Let us see to our wounded. Will you remain here, Kutar, and keep watch? If the *Marauder* returns, send a runner to me.'

The fisherman nodded. 'Aye.'

Enno hurried back to the battle ground, sparing no time for the groans of the Vikings who had been abandoned to die here.

'Tuoni!'

He found the boy lying on his side, blood streaming from his head. Ripping a strip from Kleppe's tunic, he mopped at the blood, relieved to see that the sword cut had failed to crush the cheek bone, leaving a clean, almost surgical slice. The tip of Tuoni's ear had been shaved off.

'Thank God,' murmured Enno. He grabbed a water skin from one of the Sami men and splashed it on the boy's face. Tuoni came to with a moan. 'Still with us, are you?'

'A-aye.' Tuoni struggled to sit up, helped by

276

Enno's strong arms. He raised his hand to touch his injury.

'Don't!' warned Enno. 'I'll bind the wound.'

'How bad?'

'You might not be so beautiful now, but I'm told the girls like a battle-scarred warrior. Makes you seem more interesting.'

Tuoni gave a weak chuckle. 'We won?'

'Of course.' Enno braced himself to tell the boy the news. 'But your friends are dead, I'm afraid.'

Tuoni screwed up his eyes, fighting a howl of protest. 'It was my fault.'

Enno thought there was no point avoiding the truth; Tuoni had to learn from his mistakes.

'You share the blame with them for disobeying the chief's orders—but those who killed them bear the most guilt. There was no need to murder boys. There never is.'

'Then what did they capture them for? The pirates could've kept them as slaves—alive.' Tuoni hid his eyes with his hand in case Enno saw the tears.

'I don't know why,' admitted Enno. He was just beginning to wonder.

Freydis was with the women cooking the evening

meal when she heard the news that the watchman had spotted the *Marauder* in their waters. She wished she could join Tapiola and the remaining men gathered to discuss preparations to defend the camp, but knew she would only get in the way. Instead, she retreated to her tent to pray to her gods for the safety of Enno and her Sami friends while Luonno and the other women put offerings of food and beads at the tribe's sacred spring. She would have gone with them, but her slow walk would have delayed them and all were anxious to ensure the tribe's spirit guardians were on their side in this battle. Part of her wished the Sami would just abandon the reindeer to their fate on Soroy and hide away with the rest of the tribe in their secret encampment, but she knew they could not afford to lose their herds. Why avoid a quick death in battle and replace it with slow starvation over the long winter?

'Goddess Freyja, please keep Enno safe,' she pleaded, clutching her amulet. The last time she had prayed had been in the bitter aftermath of the pirates' raid and the goddess had answered by bringing the African to her. 'I dedicate this pin to you.' Freydis took the wolf-headed pin, her most valuable possession, and laid it on the rug in front of her. 'It is yours if you bring him through this in one piece.'

Her ears caught the sound of a blade slicing through the hide-walls of the tent. Twisting round, she was confused to see a disembodied sword sawing its way to the ground.

'Who's there?' she called, her voice shaking with fear. None of the Sami owned a weapon like that. If her hip had allowed, she would have run, but all she could do was scream.

A second entrance to the tent ripped open and a Viking in a leather breastplate forced his way inside.

'Shut up or I'll kill the first person to come through that door,' the man said sharply, gesturing to the entrance that faced the central fire.

The cry died in her throat.

'Freydis Ohtheresdottir?' the man asked.

She froze.

'Come, come.' He waggled the end of his sword at her in a mocking gesture. 'The boys told us you were here before we killed them. They betrayed the location of the camp too—no wonder the old man was so sure he could give us the slip—it was damn difficult getting up here.'

'You've killed the Sami boys?' Freydis thought immediately of Tuoni. She hadn't seen him about the camp since morning.

The man laughed. 'Yes, but not before they

made a pitiful attempt to trade the information for their lives. So, thanks to them, I know exactly who you are. A very welcome and unexpected bonus.'

Freydis felt dizzy but she couldn't faint, not now. 'Who are you?'

'Sulke the Slayer, your father's enemy, as you doubtless well know.' He moved closer, his boots crushing the soft pile of the fur rug. His clothes were wet, droplets running down his legs. 'I am sorry I missed you on Bjarkoy. Your brother told me too late that you had hidden. Very clever.' He reached out and pulled her up. She swayed on her feet, hand on her hip against the bolt of pain. 'Ah, so you were injured.'

'My brother?' Her voice came out in a croak.

'Dead.'

'You . . . you killed him?'

He shook his head, his grey eyes cold. 'Ripped apart by bears at the world's end.'

She closed her eyes and gave a low moan of distress.

He tugged her towards him. 'And now, my dear, you are going to help me leave by the main path. The climb up the side of the waterfall was not pleasant and I don't think you can go that way.' He put his shoulder to her stomach and slung her over his back, arm clamped round her legs to steady her. 'Don't worry: I won't drop you unless the Sami are foolish enough to try and kill me.'

Kicking the tent flap aside, Sulke strode out into the middle of the camp. Freydis could hear the cries of distress that his appearance evoked, but she felt numb, helpless, her mind reeling. She screamed inside for Enno, but he was too far away to help her.

'Out of my way!' Sulke shouted. 'If you touch me, I'll kill the girl.'

Freydis heard Tapiola's voice beseeching him:

'Sir, I beg you, leave her be. We'll give you what you asked—reindeer, feathers, walrus ivory—name your price.'

Sulke gave an ugly laugh. 'Too late, old man, you should have treated with me when I gave you your chance. By now my men will be stripping the bones of your herd. In any case, Ohthere's daughter is too valuable to me alive. Keep your distance if you want her to stay that way.'

Sulke jogged to the path to find his way blocked by a watchman.

'Call off your dog, old man,' he sneered.

Tapiola gestured and the man reluctantly stepped aside.

'Many thanks. You have just given me the key

to my future,' Sulke called over his shoulder, waving his sword almost jauntily. And he leapt down the steep path with the sure-footed steps of a man convinced he was on the way to undisputed greatness.

21

Toki feared he had upset the beehive with his impulsive decision to ask for a particular Beorma to be considered as a future bride. With pirates to pursue, there had been no time for subtlety and he would not regret his choice—if only Aino shared his conviction that the marriage would be a good way of binding the two people with the ties of friendship, as well as a happy union for the pair of them.

On the other hand, she just might set Hero on him.

'What have you done?'

His betrothed found him helping Leif and Sigtrygger with the final preparations for the voyage south. Toki was standing in the hold with the deck planks pushed to one side, packing away the furs and other gifts the Beormas had lavished upon their new allies.

'Oh, Aino. It's you.'

To his dismay, Leif and Sigtrygger quickly made themselves scarce, leaving Aino standing on the deck with her hands on her hips, a mutinous expression on her face. Feeling at a disadvantage up to his waist in the hold, Toki climbed out to face her.

'Yes, it's me. You should have come and found me before now.'

'I know.' Toki felt his cheeks burning. He wished he had grown a beard like his father.

'So why didn't you? This whole mess is your idea, isn't it?'

He rubbed the back of his neck awkwardly. 'I thought you might be angry.'

'I am! How can you possibly think I would want to leave my home and live among you Vikings?'

'I thought . . . from what your father said, I thought you might want a chance to make a good marriage. And from what you said, the offers weren't exactly flooding in.'

'But I'm not so desperate as to exile myself from my people!' She frowned. 'So you asked for my hand out of pity?'

This time Toki spotted the bear trap before he tumbled in. 'No! I asked because I like you and I think you will make me very happy.'

284

Her face softened a little. 'Well, thank you, Toki. I like you too. But this—it's too much. I hardly know you.'

He moved closer. 'You know me well enough to be sure I won't back away from a fight—and I'll fight to keep you now I've spoken.'

'Oh.'

'And I won't ask you to change. I like your boy's leggings and the fact that you hunt as well as your brother. I even like your bear if you want to bring him with you.'

'No, no, he has to stay with the tribe.' She stopped, realizing she had given ground with that admission. Toki began to suspect that she wasn't as opposed to the idea as she would have him believe.

'The match would bring your father and brother much honour. You'd make powerful friends for your people. Isn't that better than listening to the complaints of the tribe's women that you'll never make a good match? You can rub their noses in it if you wish.'

Her mouth curled into a hesitant smile. 'There is that, I suppose.'

'And you won't be alone at home when I have to travel. There's my sister. We'll fetch her from the Finnas. You'll like her and she'll love you.' He hooked an arm around her waist, slowly reeling her in. 'So it won't be so bad, I promise.'

'But—'

'I'll bring you to visit. You are only a few weeks' sail from Bjarkoy if the winds are favourable. That really isn't so far.' They both knew it was a great distance, but for the moment the mood was to look for compromise rather than throw up difficulties. 'And your family can visit you. You'll love my island—it's much greener. More trees. Longer summers. The snow melts by spring—doesn't hang on like it does here.'

'I'll be too hot,' she complained, letting him pull her closer.

'Then I'll make you an icehouse to sit in all summer.'

'Sounds dark.'

'I'll fill it with candles for you.' He leant down and kissed the tip of her nose. 'Please, Aino, please say yes. You know I can't stay and I want to take you with me when we leave.'

She scowled. 'The chief has already agreed things with your father.'

'But I want to hear that you are willing, not that they think it is a good idea.'

She huffed out a sigh. 'All right.'

'Was that a "yes"?'

'Yes.'

He laughed and swung her round in a circle. 'You won't be sorry.'

'But you might be.' She ducked her head, embarrassed by his enthusiasm, knowing that everyone on shore was watching their discreet negotiations.

He kissed her knuckles. 'I won't be. I'm marrying the Bear Maiden, remember, the very stuff of legend. I'm expected to get a few maulings from her for my presumption in carrying her off from her family.'

She laughed at this description. 'Well then, consider yourself forewarned.'

22

Devastated, Enno did not know what to do. Ever since the messenger from Tapiola broke the news that Freydis had been kidnapped, he'd been reeling. He had not even considered that she might be a target; there had been no warning in the song. His doubts rushed back, forcing him to question if he had been a fool to trust in the Wolf Cry rather than his own plain-speaking beliefs; was he being punished for falling in love with a Viking?

If Kleppe had succeeded in gutting him as he intended, Enno doubted he could have felt worse. The thought that he'd been somewhere else when she needed him stuck in his throat like a choking fishbone.

'I should've been there,' said Tuoni. The boy had added Freydis's capture to his already heavy burden of guilt.

Enno shuddered, unable to offer comfort when he felt so bleak inside.

Tuoni dropped his head into his hands. 'Jumala or Tapio must have told Sulke the secret way up the waterfall. It's possible to approach without being seen by the guard if you don't mind getting wet.'

Enno gritted his teeth. 'There's very little that Sulke does mind. He must have tortured the boys for information; they are not to blame; they couldn't help themselves once they fell into the raiders' hands.'

'I was so mean to her,' Tuoni said at last. 'She was trying to be friends but I kept throwing in her face the fact that she was a Viking.'

'You must not talk about her as if she is dead.'

'But look what they did to Jumala! You can't expect Sulke to keep her alive.'

'Yes, I do. She has to be alive.' Enno scrubbed his wrist across his eyes, distressed to find that he was near to tears just when he had to be strong. 'Sulke made a point of taking Freydis, no one else. He must want her for something.'

'For what? A hostage? Do you think he knows that the spirit guardians talk to her?'

'I don't think that will mean anything to a man like Sulke.'

'But it means everything to my people. We've lost their messenger—they'll be angry with us. The crops will fail; calves die before they are born; the earth will turn against us.'

'Is that what they are saying?' Enno nodded to the group of Sami men who were building a rock cairn over the bodies of the fallen.

'Aye. But what can we do? We can't just leave Freydis to the raiders!'

'For the moment we have no choice.'

'We've got to do something.'

'What exactly?' Enno couldn't stop his tone being sharp. 'Have you a ship to take in pursuit and men skilled to sail it?'

Tuoni shook his head.

'To set out for the south in one of your little boats would be like setting a snail to catch a galloping horse. Our only hope is that Ohthere returns sooner than expected and is willing to go after her.'

This idea offered Tuoni new hope. 'Of course he'll give chase.'

'You do not know the man. But I'll do what's necessary to make him.'

The *Sea Otter* was far closer than Enno could have hoped or expected. It pulled into the fjord half a day behind the raiders. Tapiola had come down from the encampment to oversee the funeral rites of his people and now stood shoulder to shoulder with Enno on the little beach on Soroy, waiting for Ohthere to respond to his signal to land.

The Finna chief wrung his hands. 'How can I explain to the man that we have lost his daughter?'

'He can hardly blame you: he let his homestead be destroyed by his enemy. Your fault is small compared to his.' Enno dreaded the coming interview, but for different reasons. He was going to have to steal Ohthere's ship if he would not go to his daughter's rescue.

The *Sea Otter* moored on the beach much as the *Marauder* had done only that morning. Mingled with the gull feathers and crushed shells, blood still speckled the grit under Enno's boots— evidence of the Sami boys' suffering. More violence, endless pain as innocents were slaughtered: could these Vikings never live in peace? Enno could feel his anger rising like the sea-swell before a storm.

Ohthere jumped over the side and splashed ashore, followed by a youth and a dark-haired girl dressed in boy's leggings and tunic. The young man held her hand to help her up the beach. She laughed happily while he whispered something in her ear and pinned her short cloak with a familiar round silver brooch.

'They found him!' Tapiola clapped his hands with delight at this blessing on a day of pain. 'It's Toki, Ohthere's son.'

Ohthere strode up the short incline of the beach and threw his arms wide. 'Tapiola, my friend! You did not expect to see me so soon, no?' He crushed the old Sami leader in a hug.

'Ohthere, I have news—'

But the Viking would not let him finish. 'And look, my son! He got free and found himself a warrior bride.' He scooped Aino under one arm and swept her forward. 'My dear, this is Tapiola, leader of the Finnas.'

She nodded shyly, looking to see where Toki had gone.

Her new husband was staring at Enno in wonder. 'So this is Blue Man!' Toki exclaimed. He bounded forward and held out his hand to clasp Enno's forearm near the elbow. 'He's extraordinary! I'm envious of Freydis, Father: sure you don't want to give her that ship brooch and me this marvel?' His tone was playful, but it was plain to all that he truly did value a curiosity over silver any day.

Enno pulled his arm free, reminding himself that this was Freydis's beloved brother and he could

292

not start by thumping the Viking as he would have liked.

'Jarl, let Tapiola speak. We have urgent news, of Sulke and of Freydis,' he said sharply.

Toki raised a brow at the slave's insolent tone but Ohthere just laughed.

'What did I tell you? Freydis couldn't control a green boy, let alone this seasoned fighter. All right, Blue Man, let's hear it. We can't be far behind the pirates; we've followed their trail of slaughter and mayhem and know we are gaining on them.'

Tapiola straightened his shoulders as if preparing for a blow. 'Sulke has taken your daughter, Jarl.' He pressed in Ohthere's hand the wolf-headed pin.

'What!' Toki was the first to react, going from amused to shattered in a blink. 'How?'

'He caught two of our boys and forced them to tell our secrets. Sulke then penetrated the camp's defences when we were occupied by the attack on our herds. He threatened to kill her before our eyes if we did not let him leave with her as his hostage.'

'You let him take her alive?' Ohthere's face flushed with anger.

'We had no choice. The raiders paid heavily, losing four men, others injured; we lost a similar number, including the two boys.' Tapiola fell to his knees and pulled aside the neck of his tunic to bare his chest. 'I know my life is forfeit. We had an agreement, backed by years of faithful tribute. I promised to look after her and I meant every word. White Wolf is dear to all of us in the tribe. If you slay me, maybe our guardians will be satisfied and not punish us.'

Ohthere gripped the pommel of his sword. 'White wolf? What nonsense do you speak? What has this to do with my fool of a daughter?'

Enno growled with anger, barely restraining himself from going for the Viking's throat.

'Father,' snapped Toki, 'even you cannot blame Freydis for this!'

'She let herself be taken.'

'She was kidnapped! Like I was. Do you blame me then?'

This argument silenced Ohthere for a moment. 'No, you know I don't. I forget myself when I am angry. I apologize, Toki.'

Acknowledging his father's concession, Toki held out a hand to Tapiola. 'No one wants to kill you, sir. Please, stand up and tell us all you know about White Wolf. Is this what you call Freydis?'

Tapiola nodded. 'The guardians sent Black Wolf,' he gestured to Enno, 'and his counterpart, White Wolf, to be our protectors. She was given a song which told us that he would save us—and he has. We've not lost even one of our reindeer; we need not fear the winter. But we've lost her.'

'And I did not save her as was my duty,' added Enno. 'Your guardians were not so kind as to warn us that she was a target for this man's enemies.' He turned a stony gaze on Ohthere.

'Sulke is a plague infecting my home, my people, and now my family!' raged Ohthere. 'He must be stopped. But why take Freydis?'

'He must think you care for her,' said Enno. 'Ironic, isn't it?'

Toki shook his head. 'No, I'm afraid it isn't as simple as that. I heard Sulke talking about it; he planned then to marry Freydis if she was still alive in order to claim overlordship of our lands. She's a way for him to seize power. The pirate lords are not only fighting Harald, but also scrabbling among themselves to be the one to climb to the top of the greasy pole after the coming battle.'

'Sulke would use my daughter to secure his own position? Has he forgotten that I still stand in his way?' demanded Ohthere.

'But not for much longer, he thinks. If the rebellion is successful, he will make us outcasts, prey to any bounty-hunter. Marrying Freydis would give him a claim on Bjarkoy and our other lands.'

'I will not allow him to do this to me—to disgrace my house!'

'Worry about Freydis, not your own honour, Father.' Toki gripped Aino's hand in an unconscious gesture seeking for comfort.

'Your poor sister. We must do something,' said Aino fiercely.

'I'll disown her—let all know she's not mine so she can't inherit,' said Ohthere.

Enno took a step forward, but Toki caught him in time.

'If you do such a cruel thing, Father, to my sister, I will disown *you*. I'll take my wife back north and live there as far from you as I can go.'

Ohthere stared at his son. 'You would make me choose?'

'No, Father, it is you who is forcing me to make a choice. I can't go on watching you hurt someone I love. Freydis deserves better.'

Silence fell on the little group. Ohthere was lost for words, his old fears as difficult to eradicate as weeds in the vegetable patch, always pushing up ugly shoots of doubt.

'I am afraid,' said Enno with quiet menace, 'that this discussion is pointless without rescuing Freydis first.'

Toki dragged his eyes from his father's face.

'You are right. We have to go. Sulke will be making for the meeting of the rebels.'

Aino squeezed his hand. 'We must hurry. I fear for my sister—what she must be going through.'

Fumbling to regain some of his old authority, Ohthere nodded. 'We'll leave immediately. Either we catch up with Sulke, or at least arrive in time for the battle as King Harald ordered.' He held out a hand to Tapiola. 'Watch the north for me. I will return as soon as I can.' He flicked a glance at Enno. 'Does Blue Man stay with you? It seems no one has any control over his movements so I may as well ask.'

Enno shook his head. 'I come for Freydis, for White Wolf.' He no longer cared if the Wolf Cry song had warned that death lay on that path. He would rather go after her and challenge Sulke to give her up, even at the cost of his own life.

Tuoni stepped forward. 'Grandfather, I want to go too if you will let me. It was my fault that Sulke broke into the camp; I beg for this chance to right the wrong I did White Wolf.'

Tapiola bowed his head then looked to Ohthere for answer.

'It is a custom among my people to foster the sons of great men in other households,' Ohthere said with dignity. 'I would deem it an honour if you entrust your grandchild to me, Tapiola.'

'So be it,' agreed the chief. 'I pray you are able to take greater care of my boy than I did of your child, Jarl.'

23

Two weeks had passed since Sulke had made Freydis his prisoner. He'd carried her aboard expecting to be greeted with a hero's welcome, but instead found his crew numb with the loss of his second-in-command and repulsed from the Sami grazing grounds empty-handed. His wrath had been terrible. He berated his men as cowards, shouting that while he had single-handedly wrested their enemy's daughter from an almost impregnable camp, they had run from a bunch of herdsmen.

'But they were led by a black sorcerer, a dark elf,' protested one man, braver than the rest. 'He was not natural—skin like a starless night. He killed Kleppe—no ordinary man could have done that!'

Sulke punched the man out cold.

Freydis hugged herself, proud and relieved to hear that Enno had survived the fight.

'No matter,' Sulke announced, rubbing his grazed knuckles. 'We sail to the meeting with our brothers. Our fallen we will honour with the sacrifice of enemy blood at the great battle to come.'

The pirates had set a course for the south, cursing when the wind failed, rowing for hours to beat a tight deadline only Sulke really understood. Freydis was thankful they were so busy with preparations for this battle they talked about incessantly, honing swords and cleaning their armour; it meant she was little noticed, hunkered down among the captives from Bjarkoy. The women had greeted her with cries of distress, begging for news of their menfolk, taking heart that the crew of the *Sea Otter* had returned safely from the year-long voyage. It was Magda who offered Freydis the best comfort, telling of her brother's strange escape and the army of wild creatures he had recruited in the lands of the uttermost north. She persuaded Freydis that Sulke had lied about Toki being ripped apart by the bears, telling how her brother had appeared to be under their protection. The old nurse also confessed her weakness in betraying Freydis's existence to the pirates.

'If it weren't for me, sweeting, you wouldn't be here!' Magda said, tears slipping down her dirty cheeks.

Freydis used the end of her sleeve to wipe them away. 'If it wasn't for you, Magda, Toki would never have escaped. That puts me in your debt. Really, what happens to me doesn't matter, as long as Toki is all right.'

And as long as Enno is safe, she added silently.

But Freydis's respite among the captives did not last long. The *Marauder* met a trading vessel bound for the market of Hedeby in the land of the Danes. Seeing the chance to convert his troublesome cargo of slaves into more convenient goods, Sulke swapped the women and children of Bjarkoy for silver, keeping only Freydis in reserve.

For the first time on this voyage, Freydis found the courage to speak up before the last captive was unloaded.

'I wish to go with them, sir,' she announced as Magda was pulled from her side. She bravely grabbed the edge of Sulke's cloak to gain his attention. 'If I'm to be a captive, I wish to stay with my people.'

Sulke brushed her aside. 'Your wishes are immaterial, Ohthere's daughter.' He shoved the old woman into the small boat making the exchange between the ships. 'I have need of you, whereas they are nothing but a burden.' He gave her hand gripping his cloak an amused look, clearly expecting her

301

to enquire further. Freydis let go, lifted her chin and turned away, hoping he would not guess that she was shaking in her shoes. Her proud gesture provoked his mirth.

'Haven't you guessed, my dear? You are no captive. You have the very great good fortune of being chosen as my wife.'

She shook her head, shrinking from him. 'No.'

He ploughed on regardless. 'The ceremony will be performed as soon as we reach the meeting of my fellow leaders. Your consent is not necessary. I think I'll ask Eirik, lord of Hordaland, to stand as witness; he won't like that one bit.' His eyes swept her scornfully. 'You should be honoured. And when you are my lady, I will be able to proclaim myself legitimate ruler of Halogaland as well as my own country of Rogaland. Is that not a fine thing for your husband?'

Freydis crossed her arms defensively, chilled to the bone by this prospect.

'I'm sure my father will have something to say against your plans, sir.'

'Your father will be silenced, proclaimed a traitor, when we seize power from Harald.' He frowned as she backed away; taking a step towards her, he lowered his face to hers, speaking with bitter emphasis as his fingers curled round her neck. 'Ohthere will be hunted down like a cur so he can go and join his son among the dead. But you, my dear, will live a little longer—long enough to make sure that my claim to your home is not disputed.' With a snort of derision, he released her.

Freydis rubbed at her throat. 'But I . . . I don't want to marry you, sir.'

He stood back and smiled, but his eyes were dead. 'No, I don't suppose you do.'

Using all speed, the *Marauder* made the meeting with the other rebels only a day late. It was held near the mouth of Hafrsfjord which lay on the border between King Harald's lands and that belonging to the rebels. The fjord curved inland, a blue bite taken out of the green meadows of the flat pastures of the south-western coast of Norway, a disturbingly lush place to eyes grown accustomed to the barren lands of the north. Long grass waved on the shores, grazing for fat cattle and sheep, a blue range of mountains in the distance. Ten other warships were already there, the parties to the rebellion camped on the strand waiting for the last member of their plot. Sulke strode ashore with the strut of a barnyard cockerel, his men processing behind him bearing the goods they had stolen from Bjarkoy, the silver he had traded for the slaves, and lastly Ohthere's

303

daughter, her hair loose as Sulke had ordered. It hung like a skein of gold thread over the arm of the man who carried her.

Sulke clasped hands with a tall, red-headed Viking who came forward to greet him. The man was kitted out in oiled leather armour, the shape of a dragon's head stamped into the surface of his breast-plate and gilded with gold-leaf. He held a conical steel helmet loosely under one arm.

'Eirik! All well?'

'Sulke, you laggard! A day or two longer and we would have started without you. Harald has already gathered his fleet in the fjord. What kept you?'

'Business in the north. I took care of Ohthere for you—found him from home and dispossessed him of all he owned.' He beckoned his men to start casting the goods at his feet. They made an impressive pile: furs, ivory, jewellery, sacks of feathers, and pouches of silver.

Eirik grunted. 'That was well done. We need have no fear from that direction then?'

'No,' said Sulke firmly. 'He's a broken man, soon to be no more, off hunting for the bones of his son who I left for dead at the world's end.'

Freydis bit her tongue, though she wanted to shout that Toki had outwitted the pirate, that he was still alive. But she knew better than to do so.

'So who's that?' Eirik jerked his head at the fair-haired girl as she was placed last on the heap of goods.

Sulke crossed his arms smugly. 'Ohthere's girl.'

'He has a daughter? He kept that quiet.' Eirik frowned at the silent prisoner. He was just beginning to realize what was afoot; as currently the strongest man among the rebels, he had the most to lose if Sulke claimed overlordship of two provinces.

'I would be greatly honoured if you would witness our marriage.' Sulke gave Eirik an easy smile, daring him to refuse this courtesy before so many spectators. 'Her father has been kind enough to provide her with a dowry of everything he owns.'

Eirik answered with a strained grimace. 'Come now, Sulke. We have no time for weddings; we've a battle to fight.'

'On the contrary, we have time to seal the contract and leave the celebrations until after we've won—it will sweeten the victory even more.' Sulke's hand fell on his sword hilt, a casual gesture that fooled no one.

Eirik's eyes flicked from the ships, to the men, to the pile of goods, looking for a way out of this bind. Sulke stayed silent, enjoying every moment of his rival's discomfort.

'All right, we will witness the ceremony now,

then you can leave her here under guard until we return,' Eirik said, striving to make it sound part order, part request.

'Oh no, she'll come with me. I'm sure you understand, my friend, I would worry that some other Viking lord might steal her away when my back was turned. It is not every bride who makes her husband the richest man in the north; she is something of a prize, don't you think?'

Eirik's face clouded with barely contained anger. 'Oh, I agree, Sulke. You have the wedding mead and the sword?'

'Of course. My dear Freydis's father donated both in his absence.' Sulke snapped his fingers and one of his men came running with the goods necessary for the ceremony.

'Then get on with it. Maybe afterwards you'll let us get down to the real business—that of planning the battle.'

Freydis had been present at weddings in her village before but at her own she felt nothing more than an onlooker. After speaking some suitable words, Sulke pulled her to her feet, disguising the fact that she was crippled by keeping his arm around her waist. He thrust a goblet in her hand. Men gathered round, their expressions ranging from indifferent to hostile.

'Drink, my love,' Sulke said smoothly, forcing the cup to her lips as he announced that he was now her husband.

Next he handed her a sword. 'A gift for our first son.'

Freydis contemplated the blade—she recognized it as her father's spare. She wished she had the courage to plant it in Sulke's rotten heart.

'I know what you are thinking. Don't do it,' he murmured from behind her as he turned her round to plait her hair. This part of the ceremony should have been done by her mother or another lady from her family, but she had no one to do the task. As a married woman, she would not be permitted to wear her hair loose in public again.

This isn't happening to me, Freydis told herself. *I'm not standing in a muddy field by a fleet of warships marrying my enemy.*

But she was.

Sulke's hand rested heavily on her shoulder.

'I present my wife to you, Freydis Ohtheresdottir.'

The men cheered in a perfunctory fashion, even they sensing that the proceedings were a travesty of the joy that usually accompanied weddings.

'All right, all right, Sulke, you've got your way,' grumbled Eirik. 'Now let's stop messing around and get down to business. Stash that little bride of yours somewhere and come with us.'

Freydis gave heartfelt thanks that she was not expected to stay at her husband's side. Taking the sword from her to return it to storage, Sulke sent her back on board his ship under the guard of two of his most trusted men. Freydis wrapped herself in a spare fur and huddled in a corner of the deck, hoping no one would notice her. She thought she could bear things while she was ignored, but she was terrified of the moment when that would change.

At daybreak, the rebels' meeting finished and the leaders returned to their ships. Sulke was in excellent spirits, having been awarded a prime position in the coming battle in recognition of his new status. It made him feel more favourably disposed to his wife. After giving orders to set sail with the rest of the fleet, he beckoned Freydis to approach his position by the rudder. Reluctantly, she made her way to the stern, using the side of the ship to steady herself in the absence of her crutch. She felt very aware of the curious glances of the men working on the deck around her.

'Good morning, wife. Did you sleep well?' Sulke asked jovially.

Her sleep had been nightmarish.

'Yes, sir.'

'Have you broken your fast?'

She shook her head.

'Then we will eat together. This will be our last meal before the battle.'

She accepted the hunk of bread with a murmur of thanks. She had already decided that, if she did nothing to anger anyone, she might live long enough to find a way out of this trap.

Sulke gave her a bemused inspection, making her shudder as he tucked a stray lock of hair behind her ear.

'You're not much like your brother, are you?'

She stopped chewing.

'We had to keep him tied up and under guard at all times. You've been like a mouse, doing everything you are told without protest. Still, obedience is not a bad quality in a wife.'

She had not a shred of intention of obeying; she was merely saving her own rebellion for the most opportune moment.

'You hate me, I suppose.' It was a statement. 'Natural, considering our families have been feuding for years. But with your father and brother gone, it will end. You owe me your loyalty now.'

She owed him nothing.

He traced the curve of her cheek with a finger-tip. 'So young. I can hardly remember what it was like to be your age. Shame you're a cripple, but I suppose that's partly my fault.' He took a great bite of his own bread, speaking with his mouth full. 'I'm not such a bad man, my dear, not once you get to understand me. It has always been about honour and power. Your cursed father and that false king, Harald, style me a pirate, but it is all in the point of view of the one who speaks, is it not? To my own people, I'm a hero.'

Freydis kept her features impassive, while inwardly she snarled with scepticism.

'If you please me, I'll let you live.'

You're too kind, Freydis thought cynically.

'Why don't you speak?' He tipped her chin up, puzzled.

'I have nothing to say.'

His mouth thinned. 'You're not what I expected, I must admit. I imagined a daughter to Ohthere to be a Valkyrie, a strapping warrior maiden trumpeting her views for all to hear; not a shy dust-mote of a girl, keeping her thoughts to herself.' He tapped her forehead. 'There's more going on in there than you let on, isn't there?'

Freydis would have preferred her enemy to be dull-witted. 'If you say so.'

'Oh, I know so.' His breakfast finished, Sulke scanned the formation of ships spread out in a line across the entrance to the fjord to prevent Harald slipping past and attacking from the rear. 'All we need now is our enemy,' he mused. 'When the battle starts, I want you down in the hold out of harm's way.'

Freydis had no desire to stay on board at all. 'Could you not put me ashore and return for me later?'

Sulke patted her head in a patronizing gesture that set her teeth on edge. 'Oh no. Where I go, you follow, wife. You don't seem to realize but you are the lynchpin; without you, I might well find myself back where I started, a lesser leader among powerful men.'

Something in what he said reminded Freydis of Enno's words about her being the strand interlaced with his life; it appeared Sulke too had chosen to weave her into his story. If she tugged free, would Sulke's plans really fall? She had always thought of herself as of little importance; now it seemed she had a part to play in the future of the kingdom.

But how to snip the thread?

'Ah, there they are.' Sulke's voice resonated with satisfaction as he spotted the royal banner flying over the king's flagship. 'Harald Fairhair comes to be shaved.'

His men laughed, shouting insults and defiance as the flotilla of loyal king's men sailed up the Hafrsfjord to meet them. To Freydis, the approach was agonizingly slow, making mockery of the frantic cut and stab that would be unleashed when the two sides clashed.

'Time for you to take cover,' announced Sulke, gesturing to the compartment below the decks. It was only a few feet high; she would have to lie down to fit. A bed of furs had been spread for her and a pillow made from the embroidery she had sewn for Toki, looted during the pirates' raid on Bjarkoy.

'No, I can't!' Freydis exclaimed, seized by a growing swell of panic. To go down there would be like being buried alive.

'Do as I say!' snapped Sulke, pushing her into the hole himself. 'You'll be far safer than the rest of us.'

Freydis fell on her hands and knees, jarring her injured leg. 'Gods,' she whispered, curling into a ball. 'Help me.'

The planks were put in place over her head, leaving her in darkness. Memories of the terror of the pit on Bjarkoy rushed back—it was happening again. She had been left alone while others fought around her. Anything could occur in battle—the ship could sink or be set on fire and she would be stuck down here. Sulke had not lied when he said that her fate was bound with his: if he died, she would soon follow.

'*Ships sail into the blood-soaked dawn,*' she murmured to herself, '*souls sent to the depths.*' The song had foreseen this moment. And the churl? That must be Sulke. If so, who was his challenger? And where was he when she needed him?

'Enno,' she whispered, touching her lips to seal his name there like a kiss.

Enno stood at the prow of the *Sea Otter* watching the enemy ships disappear into the still waters of Hafrsfjord, a light breeze making their movements slow and deliberate like a pod of whales heading for their feeding grounds. It was hard to believe it was the opening moves in a battle for life or death.

'Can you see the *Marauder*?' asked Toki, coming to stand beside him. The two had become friends over the weeks' voyage, united by their love for Freydis.

'Aye, she's there in the centre.'

Toki shaded his eyes to scan the shore. 'Where's Freydis? Do you think Sulke will have put her on land somewhere? He wouldn't want her in battle, would he?'

'Surely she would only be in the way? The last thing he would want is his claim to Halogaland killed by a stray arrow. She should be safe somewhere.'

'So how will we find her?'

Enno raised his hands and let them drop helplessly. 'We can't. But your father has given his word he will fight for Harald. If we add our strength to the others, and defeat Sulke and his allies, then we will be helping free Freydis.'

Toki gazed vengefully after the rebel fleet. 'Then let us send them all down to the depths and end this.'

'I'd prefer to take at least one of his crew alive to find out what Sulke has done with your sister and the rest of your people.'

Toki searched the deck of the ship for Aino, spotting her sitting quietly to starboard. She was plucking the string of her bow thoughtfully.

'I must make sure my wife is secure before we join the battle.'

'She won't like that.' Enno had already come to like the spirited Beorma girl who was the only person on the ship who dared tease Ohthere.

'I won't be giving her a choice.'

It was better not to get involved in this argument. 'Then I suggest you leave her on the nearest islet with a small boat. That way she won't be stranded if anything happens to us. I will tell Tuoni to guard her—I have no more stomach to take a boy into the battle than you your wife.'

Aino was outraged when she received her orders.

'I'm not going,' she told her husband. 'I'm the bear maiden, remember, not a parcel to be left for later collection!'

'No, you are our last line of defence.' Toki hugged Aino tightly to him. 'If we fail, it will be your duty to find Freydis and retreat to the safety of your people. And Tuoni, can I trust you to help her do this?'

The boy nodded soberly.

Aino got her arm free and pounded Toki's chest. 'You—are—not—to—die! You understand me? You have to promise you won't do anything stupid like getting yourself killed.'

Toki hid his smile in her hair. She was a fierce one, his Beorma bride. 'I wouldn't dare.'

'Good.' She pulled away, holding herself proudly. 'Just you remember that.'

After finding an island safe haven for Aino and Tuoni, the *Sea Otter* left them and hurried to join forces with King Harald. Toki did not join the watch at the prow of the ship as they strained to see which side fortune was favouring in the battle; he stood at the stern, eyes on the tiny figure of his wife until she was out of sight.

24

A battle on water. Freydis had never really understood what that meant for those in the ships, but now she knew. The noise was the worst: pounding feet, curses, clashing metal, screams, the screech of wood against wood as the ships collided. She thought she heard men boarding the vessel from the starboard side. The ship lurched as weight shifted one way. More intense clashing; cries; the smell of smoke.

'Please, Freyja, anything but fire,' she prayed.

Something dripped on her from above—water but with a strange tang that she feared was blood. How much longer?

Then Sulke's crew started chanting and thumping their shields: 'Thar! Thar! Thar!'

They cried the name of one of the leaders, renowned as a fierce berserk. The story had

317

circulated the rebel camp that he was able to clear a deck of men without a stroke landing on him as if blessed with invisible protection by the gods. The crew urged Thar on with whoops and insults to the men on the king's flagship.

Suffocating in darkness, terrified of what was happening, Freydis decided she couldn't bear not knowing, even if she was punished for her disobedience. Gingerly, she pushed up a corner of one of the deck planks. There was no one near but the man on the rudder; the crew had all rushed to the middle of the boat to watch Thar's attempt on Harald's vessel. Her exit was hidden by the body of one of the failed boarders. He lay in a twisted heap, neck broken.

Staying low, Freydis edged to the side. Not far away, on the calm waters of the fjord, a ship's sail burned like parchment tossed in a fire, flames creeping up the rope webbing, consuming the cloth, smoke billowing like storm clouds. Men were leaping from the doomed vessel and swimming for shore. She could not tell if they were friend or foe.

A casualty floated by in the water, face down. He bobbed past, looking absurdly peaceful in comparison to the violent action on board the ships.

If she jumped while no one was looking, would she make it to shore? Freydis hadn't tried swimming since her injury and doubted the leg would be of much use, but perhaps she could manage. It was better than waiting here to die.

She was about to take her chance when a great roar went up from Sulke. He was pointing back out to open sea at a square-sailed ship bearing down on them. The sweeps were out: oars beating the water in perfect time.

'It's the *Sea Otter*! Thank be to Tyr: he's sent me my enemy to destroy in our hour of victory. To the benches!'

The crew rushed to their positions, two men to each oar. Deftly, the helmsman steered the *Marauder* in a circle. All Sulke's fighters knew that Ohthere's ship was theirs to conquer—their leader would have it no other way.

Freydis shrank behind the fallen man, her plan rapidly changing. Far better than drowning in the attempt to swim to the distant shore would be a short dash for her father's vessel. She just had to wait for them to be close enough.

Sulke spoiled her chance by striding to the stern to take over the rudder. He immediately noticed her in her hiding place and gave a cruel, excited laugh.

'Come to witness the end of your worthless father, my dear?' He pointed to the planks beside him. 'Stand here. I promise you'll have a good view.'

He seized her wrist with his free hand and pulled her closer. 'Just think: in a few minutes you'll come into your inheritance.'

'What are you going to do?' she asked, horrified as the two ships showed no sign of giving up their collision course.

'Ram him, of course!' crowed Sulke. 'His round-bottomed keel might be good for trading, but it doesn't stand a chance against a fighting dragon ship. We'll go through his side like a stab to the heart.'

Freydis couldn't help herself. 'I hate you,' she spat, but that only made Sulke laugh. Horror-struck she watched the ship approach, her father directing from the prow, the men straining on the benches, and even a familiar gangly figure on the rudder.

Toki.

Gods, it had been so long—and there he was alive and well.

Then she saw Enno at his side and she wanted to fly to him, put an end to the terrible separation from him.

'You must stop this!' she demanded, tugging at Sulke's hand on the rudder, sinking her nails into his skin.

Sulke was amused, rather than offended by her defiance. 'So the mouse shows her teeth.' He shoved her away. 'I'm so glad you are warming to me, my dear.'

She couldn't let this happen. Where was the churl's challenger? Surely this was his moment?

But the song had not said who or what the challenger was. With a flash of insight, Freydis realized that it could just as well be her. Yet what could she do—one girl against a ship of battle-hardened Vikings? Not fight them—that was out of the question. There had to be some weakness she could exploit.

Watching Sulke steer, an answer came to her. The rudder. As the daughter of a ship-builder she knew that if you took out the stave attaching the handle to the paddle in the water, you disabled the ship. Just like Sulke had done to her when he denied her a crutch.

Still, it would be no easy task—and would probably mean her death whether she succeeded or failed. But that didn't matter—not if she could save Enno and her family. The gods had given her power after weeks of helplessness. This was her moment.

Looking about her, Freydis saw that the tool she needed was tantalizingly close—an axe held limply in the hand of the dead man. Would she have time to reach it and get in the two or three blows she would need to damage the rudder stem? That was a question she couldn't answer without making the attempt.

Sulke unwittingly helped her by choosing this moment to shout to his crew.

'Faster, men! Put your backs into it!'

As the ship lurched, Freydis pretended to stagger and fall to her knees, grabbing the axe in the folds of her skirt.

The tempo of the oars increased, foam flying from the dragon-headed prow. Sulke ignored his clumsy wife, intent on the tricky manoeuvre of steering the ship so it would look as if he was aiming to come alongside for boarding, while intending to force a collision at the last moment. Oars would break, men be thrown into the water; the deck of the *Sea Otter* would be plunged into complete confusion, locked in the jaws of her rival. He threw his head back and laughed.

Thump.

At first, Sulke didn't realize what had happened; he looked to the *Sea Otter* for the source of the missile he thought had landed on his ship's flank.

Crack.

Movement behind him caught his eye—his wife was tugging an axe free of the rudder shaft to bring it down for a third quick blow. The wood splintered. Sulke made a grab for the axe with his free hand and wrestled it from her with no difficulty.

'What have you done?' he bellowed at her.

As he spoke, he felt the handle of the rudder beneath his palm slide, swinging free. No longer connected to the drag of the steering paddle, it flapped aimlessly. The *Marauder* began to veer in the wrong direction, away from the *Sea Otter*. With a furious yell, Sulke struck Freydis to the deck with a clumsy left-handed blow from the axe; he then struggled to control his ship, but it was no good, the rudder paddle was stuck, steering the ship in circles.

'Something's happened to Sulke's ship!' exclaimed Toki.

'Prepare for boarding!' ordered Ohthere, not pausing to wonder at this gift from the gods. Judging the drift of the *Marauder*, he steered his own vessel skilfully alongside, using his prow to shatter oars and catapult rowers into the water.

Enno and Toki were the first to leap the short distance between the boats, men of Bjarkoy at their backs, all thirsting for revenge. Sulke's men ran to meet them, but they also had to fight the carnage the ramming from the *Sea Otter* had left on deck—oars on the portside scattered like tree-trunks felled in a hurricane.

Shoulder to shoulder, Enno and Toki fought their way up the deck, heading for the man defending his position by the rudder. Only a few paces from their goal, a rebel jumped into Toki's path, forcing him to engage at close-quarters, so it was Enno who reached Sulke first.

The pirate's eyes widened when he saw the dark elf-man charging him. He parried Enno's first strike; the blade slid to bite into the ship's rail, gouging a chunk from the smooth timber.

'What kind of man are you?' snarled Sulke.

'An angry one,' spat Enno. 'What have you done with Freydis?'

'You mean my little wife?' Sulke slashed at Enno's unprotected left side; the blow barely reached as the African managed to step back in time. Only the tip dug into his ribs, drawing blood that trickled down his side to join that which had already been spilt on the deck, making footing treacherously slick. 'She lies at my feet. The girl thought she could challenge me, but she's met with her reward.'

For a fatal moment, Enno's attention wavered to the small figure huddled by the ship's side. Sulke took advantage of his shock, lunging forward to plant his sword in the African's stomach. But his own deeds thwarted him: foot slipping in the blood he had already shed, he went down and the strike fell awry.

Enno's did not. He buried his sword in Sulke's back, pinning him to the deck. The man shuddered, fingers clawing at the planks, then went still.

Having defeated his opponent, Toki ran to Enno's side. He looked down at the pirate leader. 'Dead?'

'I sincerely hope so,' panted Enno. He stepped over the body to reach Freydis. He felt for a pulse in a worryingly cold neck.

'My sister's here?' Toki rushed to help Enno lift the body. 'Gods! What's wrong with her?'

Enno was frantic. 'She's still alive, but I can't see her injury. There's so much blood.'

'Quickly! Take her back to our ship.'

Enno swung her up into his arms, cuddling her protectively to his chest. As they passed across the deck, it was clear that the battle was almost over. Sulke's men were either dead or fleeing, throwing their weapons away in a bid to swim for shore. Enno carried Freydis to the *Sea Otter* and laid her on a pile of clean furs. Still she hadn't uncurled, nursing some hidden wound, but Enno couldn't help but hear her laboured breathing.

'Freydis, it's me.'

Her pale eyelashes flickered open. 'Enno?'

He leant forward and kissed her brow. 'We'll make you better, don't worry.'

Toki knelt at her other side. 'I'm here too, Freydis. Everything's going to be all right.'

Ohthere crouched beside his son, awed by the bravery of the child he had treated so badly. She'd risked herself for them all. 'How is she?' He tentatively touched his daughter's wrist.

Toki moved aside the cloth she had clutched to her stomach and saw the wound for the first time.

'She's dying,' he said thickly.

'No!' protested Enno, but he knew from one glance that they could do nothing for her. The axe had struck too deeply. 'No.'

Ohthere's blue eyes glazed with tears as he studied the pale face of his youngest child. 'You were very brave, my daughter,' he whispered. 'You did not run. But this time I wish you had.'

Freydis's lips quivered into a fleeting smile.

'I'm so proud of you.' He placed his hand on her forehead in a sign of blessing, claiming her as his once and for all. 'I'm sorry.'

Toki held her hand close to his chest. 'Don't leave us, Freydis. I want you to meet Aino—I'm married—I never got the chance to tell you. You'll like her—she has a bear and knows lots of new stories.'

'That's . . . good.' Freydis's eyes shifted to Enno. She whispered something but he couldn't quite catch it. He bent closer so her lips grazed his ear.

'I'm sorry—I snipped the thread.' Her words were like gossamer, barely there as they floated on her last breaths. 'Had to.'

Tears streamed down Enno's cheeks. 'Freydis, my White Wolf,' he murmured as he brushed the hair from her face. 'God be with you.'

'Enno.' She was fading, life running out with the blood from her veins. 'Weave a new life—please.'

'I only wanted you.' His voice broke into sobs.

'You must live . . . for me.' She clutched at his hand, knowing she had to stay until she had won this last promise from him.

'I will, my love. Wait for me at the other end of the rainbow bridge to the next world. I'll come and find you.'

Freydis smiled, and let herself drift away, escaping the claws of pain for peace.

HOMECOMING

'Like a stream fast flowing,
sorrow, the death of laughter,
through the brow's white woods,
forces tears down into her lap.
The snake-lair's goddess,
her weeping eyes swollen
with bitter fruits, looks to me,
Odin's craftsman, for consolation.'

(GISLI SURSSON'S SAGA)

25

They buried Freydis in the hull of Sulke's ship on the island at the mouth of Hafrsfjord. Ohthere placed her wolf-headed pin on her breast and her brother folded the embroidery she had sewn for him under her head. Aino covered the sister she never got to meet with a white bear skin and Tuoni gave her a reindeer comb.

Tears running unheeded down his cheeks, Toki used the Sami's gift to unbind his sister's butter-yellow hair, combing it loose to remove all claim on her in the afterlife by her false husband.

King Harald and his house-karls were celebrating the routing of his pirate enemies at a feast on the mainland but none of Ohthere's household had any desire to join them. No one wanted to relive the sinking of Eirik's ship, the death of Thar the Berserk, and defeat of the other rebel lords. Instead, Leif and the other singers in the crew chanted a lament long into the night while Sigtrygger served Freydis's favourite food in her honour. They did not forget Freydis watching from the afterlife, leaving her with a sack of grain and other supplies to take with her to Freyja's hall in Folkvangar.

With a bitter taste in his mouth, Enno stood alone at the sea's edge and gazed across at the fires of the celebration. His heart felt as if it had been carved from his chest. What had it all been for? A gang of petty leaders defeated to elevate one man to undisputed kingship so he could claim tax and tribute. Nothing in that was worth Freydis's life.

Leaving Ohthere keeping watch at his daughter's grave, Tuoni, Toki, and Aino came to stand either side of Enno.

'I thought I was the challenger,' Enno said when he realized who was there with him. 'I was ready to forfeit all as the song said.'

'But so was she,' replied Tuoni. The experience of the last weeks had made great changes to him; he'd left home a boy, now he was a young man, his wisdom earned the hard way. He gripped Enno's forearm in sympathy. 'White Wolf fought for her pack and won. My people will remember her in our songs—we will remember you both.'

Toki pulled Aino closer, needing the promise of love and life that she now represented in the chill winter of his grief for his sister. 'My father is sailing after the slave traders but Aino and I are going back to Bjarkoy to look after our people. Tuoni will live with us until it is time for him to return to his own tribe. You are welcome to come with us if you wish.'

Enno had no wishes. He held his hands empty at his side.

'What will you do now, Blue Man?' persisted Toki. 'My sister's death means you are free.'

'I do not want my freedom at such a price.'

'I know, but take it—she would have freed you in any case. Let it be her gift to you. She would have wanted something good to come out of all this bloodshed.'

'Will you go to your home?' asked Aino gently.

Enno turned his gaze to the south, imagining all the leagues that lay between him and the place of his birth and the people there that no longer knew him. He then thought of Tuoni, Tapiola, and the people of his adopted tribe; of Freydis's brother and his wife, the daughter they would one day have who would be named after the girl who saved them during a battle. Freydis had made him promise to carry on without her, foreseeing how lost he would now feel. He had to honour her last request, though it felt as if it was killing him. To live again, he had to be among those who had known her. His own hopes were in ruins; like Bjarkoy, he had to rebuild.

'No, I won't head south.' He met their eyes, brushing away his tears. 'My pack is here now. But as I am to stay, please, call me Enno.'

Glossary

Asgard: home of the gods

Balder: god renowned for his beauty

Bifrost: rainbow bridge to world of gods

Dirham Coins: silver coins imported from the Middle East

Fenrir: the great wolf, son of Loki

Folkvangar: goddess Freyja's hall in Asgard to which her followers go in the afterlife

Freyja: goddess of fertility

Hel: monstrous daughter of Loki

Jormungand: serpent that circles the world

Kalma: Sami goddess of death

Loki: trickster god, often guilty of evil deeds

Nakki: Sami water-spirit

Nidhogg: dragon that chews on the roots of the tree of life

Norns of the Well of Urd: the Viking fates; they guard the spring at the root of the tree of life

Odin: foremost god; god of battle, poetry, and death

Ragnarok: the battle at the end of time

Rot: Sami god of the underworld

Sami: people of the north of Norway and Finland

Skald: bard or story-teller

Surma: Sami monster, symbol of violent death

Surt: giant who will set the world on fire at Ragnarok

Thor: god of sky and thunder

Tribute: money or goods given to an overlord or protector

Tyr: god of war

Ukko: Sami god of the heavens

Valkyrie: beautiful women who roam battlefields choosing the warriors worthy to be taken back to Valhalla

Julia Golding is the author of over ten books for children. Her stories are set all over the world (and in some new worlds too) and span the centuries.

In her first year as a published author, she won a Nestlé Gold Prize, was shortlisted for the Costa Children's Book Award, longlisted for the prestigious Carnegie Medal, and won the Waterstone's Children's Book Prize.

Julia Golding lives in Oxford with her husband and three children. *Wolf Cry* is her seventh novel for Oxford University Press.